Naomi Blue

Naomi Blue
A Novel

By

Jody G. Russell

North Star Press of St. Cloud, Inc.
St. Cloud, Minnesota

Copyright © 2010 Jody G. Russell

Cover art by Joel Cooper.
Author photo by Steve Rohlf.

ISBN-13: 978-0-87839-387-9

All rights reserved.

This is a work of fiction. Names, characters, places, and incidents are the products of the author's imagination or are used fictitiously. Any resemblance to actual events or persons, living or dead, is entirely coincidental.

First Edition, July 2010

Printed in the United States of America

Published by
North Star Press of St. Cloud, Inc.
P.O. Box 451
St. Cloud, Minnesota 56302
northstarpress.com

Dedication

Although writing is something I do as a solitary experience as a way of letting the noise in my head tumble out onto the computer screen in the form of words and paragraphs, it's much easier to do with the support of family and friends. To all of you who let me talk on and on about fictional Naomi Blue, who didn't mind when I rushed home to write rather than sit over another cup of coffee, or who let me off the hook when it came to cooking dinner, thank you.

Chapter One

Naomi Blue

It was the heaviest bed in the store. It took four men to haul the dark oak frame up the narrow flight of stairs to her room. They had heaved and sweat, grunting and muttering until they had reached the top landing. Naomi Blue had waited at the bottom, watching them strain, feeling slightly guilty at having bought the bed in the first place, uncomfortable at the effort required to bring the bed up, even though she had paid fifty dollars for the service.

For two weeks before, she had slept on the floor in an old drab-green, fleece-lined sleeping bag as she worked at the bakery to earn a little more money so that she could pay off the cost of a box spring and mattress.

When the bed began to vibrate it was an early warning sign of the impending crescendo of the train horn. She lay on her back and felt the bed shiver and shake. As usual, the small blue vases on her dresser shifted forward until they were halfway to the edge. It was a medium-sized train this time. The heavier freights, car upon car, rhythmically passing behind the house, could shimmy the vases right onto the floor.

Naomi Blue laid on her back and felt the train, experienced the train actually, counting the cars as best she could in her mind, letting the blaring horn float through her consciousness. Thirty-five cars plus the engine, she thought, as the sound finally receded and she drifted into a restless sleep, knowing that it was nearly time to get out of bed, set the vases back in place, and go to work.

The house was small and had more charm from the outside than from the inside. The large front porch and freshly painted facade had pleased Naomi Blue from the first moment she'd passed it and seen the for-sale sign. The slate-blue shingles and newly painted dark-burgundy trim and shutters were warm and inviting, reminding her of a house on the beach on the Atlantic, not a midwestern town far from salt water. When the widow Wanda Cooper had decided it was time to move from the house, she'd asked her son and daughter-in-law to spiff it up. They had used little imagination painting the interior walls antique white but had put some energy into what Mona Derkins called front yard curb-appeal. Mona Derkins was the realtor whose name appeared on weekly ads in the paper as "the realtor who knows where home is." The upstairs was little more than a bedroom and small closet. Downstairs, built-in cupboards in the dining room and kitchen gave the house charm reminiscent of a time when craftsmen designed a house with individual flair and a distinctive style. Hardwood floors in the living dining room transitioned to yellow speckled linoleum in the kitchen. The last time there had been serious work done to the house was in 1947, but Naomi Blue didn't much care. It was a place to put her bed.

The easement between the tracks and the property line was inconsequential. She could count the railroad ties from her bedroom window. Clearly this was the reason the house had stood vacant for over a year. Mona Derkins hadn't mentioned the train tracks, but one look at the back and there was no need to say too much anyway. A small storage shed was hidden amongst vines and weeds in the far corner of the yard. A couple of small gnarled apple trees suggested fruit in the fall and one had a weathered birdhouse hanging amid the leaves. Mona Derkins hadn't located the key to open the padlock on the shed door, but assured Naomi that it would show up in due time. On the south side of the shed were the gardens. Naomi Blue had let these gardens, once carefully maintained by the widow, become what Naomi called "natural." Wild grasses and thistle took root, along with goldenrod that shot up through the weeds to glow in the morning dew. Naomi Blue liked the disorganized look, and hoped eventually to be able to identify all the prairie grasses and native plants that grew there, but never to actually cultivate it. Gardening wasn't something she thought sounded like much fun. She was glad Wanda Cooper had moved to Florida and wouldn't be witnessing her negligence. From the back door, the gardens provided a visual buffer from the train tracks—at least when the twice a day freight wasn't passing through.

Naomi Blue shook off her dream, which bordered her reality too closely for her to want to stay within. She frequently closed her eyes to return to an arousing misty image, trying to conjure up another episode in the flow of the dream. These days, though, it was hard to shed sleep since she found less appeal in the reality of her life.

Naomi slid out from her covers, pulling the blanket up over the sheets. She barely left a trace in the bed, sleeping so still in one place. The floor was cold, so she hopped from one wool throw rug to another to grab her clothes from the small chair with the loose leg she'd found in front of someone's house, ready for the trash. It might not hold her weight if she sat on it but it worked fine to drape her clothes on at night. Yesterday's clothes were good enough for now, Naomi thought. They usually were.

The morning sun was shining in through the vertical windows that ran alongside the front door. Dust beams landed on the lower steps. Naomi opened the door, flooding light into the house, hoping to find the Friday newspaper tossed close to the door. She searched the overgrown shrubs in front of the porch wondering if there was some personal meaning in the location of the paper. Did he toss it away from the door on purpose or was he just a poor shot? Naomi stepped out on the porch, her bare feet scratched by the bristle mat whose sole purpose had proven to be a warm place for the neighborhood tabby. Naomi saw the paper directly in front of the nameless overgrown prickly shrub. She bent over to grab the paper, thinking wryly that it took a whole week for the town of Copper Prairie to come up with twenty-eight pages of news and gossip.

With the coffee brewing, Naomi leaned her elbows on the rickety kitchen table to glance through the *Copper Press*. Small town papers served important civic functions and Naomi Blue wanted to know it all, as if somehow the mere reading of it would make her part of the community. After living in the house for a few months, she was still virtually unknown in town. Yet, she knew whose children were engaged to who, what young couple had had their first baby, and what older couple had been surprised by their fifth. She knew who was to be buried in the Lutheran cemetery down the dusty dirt John Moore Road. She knew when the Rotary club was having its annual pancake breakfast and the Lions Club its hosta plant sale (three varieties even). She knew that the city council was changing its monthly meeting from the first Tuesday of the month to the second in November because of Election Day, same time, same place. Naomi skimmed through the help-wanted ads, looking for something new, something different, something she could do that might change her life. She read through the for-sale listings, wondering if there might be something she could afford for her still relatively unfurnished house. And she read through the wanted listings, wondering if she might own something someone else might want, to give her a bit more money than she earned in the bakery. Nothing.

Friday was generally a busy day at the bakery. Naomi Blue imagined it was because of folks getting treats for their weekends, their friends, and their families. Just once she would like to go into a bakery and ask for a dozen of those famous sweet rolls, which won first prize in a bake-off at the county fair in 1957 and have been sought after ever since. She went upstairs for a clean pair of white pants and the pink t-shirt from Ida's Bakery showing the outline of a stout woman with a long braid, clearly Ida. She was holding a rolling pin in one hand and a coffee cup in the other, her braid curling upwards as if in motion. She didn't much mind the t-shirt, despite it being pink, because the apron covered most of the graphic, except for the peeking out of the rolling pin on one side, the mug on the other and the tip of her braid up towards the neckline. Ida herself was hidden, thankfully, because Naomi's idea of an attractive shirt didn't include a drawing of a woman heavier than herself.

IDA MINSKY

IDA PATTED HER HANDS DOWN on her apron, leaving small yet pudgy white handprints. It was already seven o'clock and her one employee, that girl with the odd name, was not in sight. *Hard work, hard work,* she thought, *that's what it takes to get somewhere. That's what it takes, yes, put your past behind you, get on with life, don't look back. No, don't look back. Work hard. Save for the future. Be on time.*

Ida was sure about these sorts of things in the way that the accumulation of too many hard years makes one sure of things. *It's what I've done. I've worked hard. That girl,* she thought, *where is that girl?* Ida came around from behind the counter to look out the window to the street. No sign of her. "That girl," she said aloud. "I'm talking to myself now? Ach. I'm getting old."

Ida went back to check on the apple cheese ring cakes that were still in the oven. *My favorite,* she thought. *Give me a slice of that and a cup of fresh coffee. Yes, that is a piece of happiness, a piece of happiness indeed.*

The bells attached to the door jangled, and Ida was relieved to see Naomi Blue coming in, the pink shirt stretched too tight across her chest, the girl shivering off the cold. Didn't she have a coat? It was October. In this part of Minnesota that meant snow could come any time, any time now. Where was this girl's coat? Ida didn't say anything, turning away as she came in as if she hadn't been waiting.

"Brr," Naomi said. "It's a bit cold this morning. I didn't realize it because the sun is so bright."

Ida glanced back towards Naomi, sliding the last tray of cakes from the oven. Hmph. Though she was glad that Naomi Blue had managed finally to arrive, she didn't want her to think she was needed, so important that the world started upon her arrival, that nothing had happened in the bakery so far, despite the fact that Ida had been rising yeast and turning the dough since 4:30 that morning. No, the girl should not think her arrival mattered so much to Ida. But of course it did.

Naomi grabbed a clean white apron from the linens drawer, pulled it over her head and began to wrap the ties around her waist and back again. The knot ended up in the front. Ida took great pleasure in the image of the girl, the clean whiteness of her clothes, the contrast of the shirt. She couldn't hire any boys to work for her. It wasn't likely they would wear that pink, but that was just fine with her. She didn't trust the boys at the register, didn't want them alone in the store with her, she was just fine with girls, and even then she sometimes didn't trust them. This Naomi Blue seemed trustworthy, and she didn't complain about hefting the large sacks of flour and sugar that came in through the back door on Monday mornings.

Ida couldn't resist the scent of the apple cake, not today anyhow, thinking how much she deserved it, this morning treat.

Barely letting it cool, she sliced up the first one out of the oven. A slice for Naomi and a slice for her. Without yet really greeting the girl, without even really acknowledging her with more than a throaty, "Hmph," Ida offered her a piece of warm cake.

"Fantastic. Thanks, Ida. This looks good, so golden on top. Did you do something different?"

"Same. Same as it's been. Same as I've always done. Longer than you've been on this earth, I imagine."

"Probably," Naomi agreed, clearly not wanting to disagree with her employer. "Probably so." They ate standing behind the counter, with a few satisfied, "Mmms," apiece.

Ida watched the girl devour the cake, wondering if she'd eaten anything else that morning, or if the cake was indeed as delicious to her as it was to Ida herself. This recipe was one of the few that she had written down, many years ago it was, fearful that she'd forget them, these treasured recipes, one of her mother's recipes. In fact, even then she had not recalled the correct amount of cinnamon or baking powder, and so had tried it with varying amounts of both until the combination created the cake of her memory, rising just high enough not to be thought of as a torte. Memory of taste, Ida knew, was as accurate as other senses.

The bakery was a fixture in the town of Copper Prairie, one of those shops a town needs, like the grocery store or the hardware store, important to its daily life, but not a gathering place. That reputation had belonged to McNeill's Drugstore, which once was more than a place to get throat lozenges, with its green vinyl-covered stools that were bolted to the floor and had great momentum as they spun completely around, letting you face the long Formica counter at one moment and the shelves of shaving cream the next. McNeill's was once known for its hamburgers cooked with a spatula on a greasy grill and a cherry coke served with a red-and-white striped straw. The grill had long ago been replaced by increased display space, now home to the "natural and organic" section. This was a town with two main streets, running parallel to each other, barely half a mile in length. Between Main Street and Carriage Boulevard were a handful of connecting roads. The town had two bars, both a little more rough than pretty, though one had live music and the other a vintage juke box filled with oldies and a smattering of disco. Down the street from Ida's was the Carriage General, a musty-smelling store that sold everything from clothes and steel-toed boots to teak salad bowls and crystal-like wine glasses. Robinson's Grocery was towards the end of Main Street. Rooster Robinson took the store over from his parents, who ran it after Rooster's grandfather died overseas in the First World War. Ida kept her distance from Rooster, a man as ornery as his nickname implied. Of course, she was one of the few people who knew his real name was Roger, but calling him by that name would increase the likelihood of conflict.

Ida lived above the bakery in a small apartment, accessible from a staircase at the back of the shop. She was never far from her cinnamon, butter, and sacks of flour. Upstairs she kept a chair in the front window that overlooked Carriage Street, sitting in it on the rare occasions the bakery wasn't open and she was awake.

The door opened with a gust of wind that blew leaves into the bakery along with a young man. Ida turned from the oven to be sure he would close the door. It was a constant irritant to Ida that so many customers these days left it open. Her heating bill was low, and she wanted to keep it that way. The bells clanged one more time as he shut the door. Very good. Ida waited for Naomi Blue to greet him. Within ten seconds of entering the store, greet the customer, she'd told Naomi on her first day. Make the customer feel welcome. Happy customers buy more.

Naomi didn't disappoint Ida. "Hi, can I help you?"

"Hi. Yes. Where did that wind come from? Wow, it sure is blowing."

"Yeah, it sure is," Naomi responded.

Ida listened carefully. She was critical about such things, critical about how her employee interacted with customers, if she was friendly enough, or too friendly. This one, this Naomi, tended to be quiet. But she had good eye contact with people and kept focused.

"Uh, let's see. I'm not sure what I want . . . something that will go well with coffee."

"How about one of our famous sweet rolls?"

"That sounds great."

Naomi Blue

Naomi Blue served the guy who had come into Ida's, aware mostly that he had the kind of dark-brown eyes that she had more than once before mistakenly attributed to warmth of heart. She was polite, courteous, and nothing more. With Ida listening to her constantly, she was usually cautious about what she said. Naomi knew Ida listened because she could sometimes see her out of the corner of her eye, head cocked, ear towards the front of the store, clearly listening, despite the fact that she might be involved with an enormous quantity of dough. Naomi knew there was a certain amount of distrust exuding from Ida towards her, but she dealt with it the only way she could—by ignoring it. Perhaps over time, it would dissipate.

The guy took his coffee and sweet roll to one of the tables near the window. Naomi busied herself cleaning the counter near the register. There were two types of solo customers, she had determined. There were the ones who were busy with a newspaper, a book, or their own thoughts, and sat and enjoyed their food. And then there were the kind of customers interested in talking, perhaps lonely, perhaps just needing a change of place, and came in more for the company than for the bakery goods. Naomi had turned it into a game trying to type the person quickly. This guy was the solitary quiet sort, she predicted. She was wrong.

"I haven't been here for a while, been out of town for a few years. I haven't seen you here before."

"No," Naomi replied. "I'm new."

"How long have you been working here?"

"Some months." Naomi didn't offer much in her answers, she was very aware of that.

"Ah."

The guy turned back to his coffee, looked out the window. Perhaps Naomi had been spared more conversation.

Henry Alexander

It had been a long time since he'd been in Ida's Bakery and had only come in as part of his plan to reconnect himself with the town. He began by driving past the Copper Prairie Central School, where he'd been a student from grades seven through twelve. Then he drove past the elementary school. He had gotten out of the car to walk around the building and found himself standing before the monkey bars, wondering if he could finally work his way across them without the ache in his arms. Hoping no one was around to see him, he grabbed onto them, bent his knees, and swung one rung at a time the six feet to the other side. It had been a long time ago since the teasing. Some things don't leave a person, he thought. He made it, though his arms still ached.

Henry walked the downtown streets, seeing what had changed, what was the same. It surprised him that so much was the same. There were a few new stores and a few new owners. But Copper Prairie still felt familiar. Since he'd come back, he had been living off his savings and spending a bit too much time in the bars. Maybe it wasn't too much, but he was spending more time in them than he ever had in the past. He was now quite at home on the bar stools in Mikey's, which could give you a splinter if you gripped the seat at all. The drinks were two for one on Thursdays, and free for women on Fridays. It didn't matter to him, he went both days, and never with a date. Saturday nights he went to the Ringworm, which had live music pushed deep in the back dark corner. If the band had drums, the route to the bathroom would inevitably be blocked. You didn't want to have to get there too quickly. It wasn't unusual to see someone carelessly sway into the cymbals. Still, the dark and boozy atmosphere was one Henry liked. He could escape and yet be a part of something he'd never been a part of in Copper Prairie.

Ida's was the best place—actually the only place—in town for a good cup of coffee. He was passionate about his coffee. When he lived in Minneapolis he had bought it freshly roasted. The first time he'd bought it at the corner on the street near the university, he hadn't realized that it was whole bean. He'd stuck it in his backpack and had gotten home before he realized it wasn't ground. He went back out and bought an expensive grinder just so he could drink this pound, too self-conscious to return to the coffee shop. It turned into a routine with a distinct hint of snobbery in his demands for freshly roasted and ground beans. Every morning he'd grind his beans and make French press, drinking the whole carafe while reading the paper. He felt no shame in his elitism. If he wanted to drink coffee and people-watch, there were many interesting coffee shops in Minneapolis, and he could go from one favorite to another, depending on his mood. And he could cross the river to St. Paul if the Minneapolis locales became too dull. Copper Prairie was another thing entirely. There was just Ida's, unless you counted the gas station that served up bitter coffee in twenty-four-ounce Styrofoam cups with plastic pull-back lids. And so he sat there looking out the window, peering down Carriage Boulevard, watching the wind blow leaves and old plastic bags up into the air. Not because that was so interesting, but because it was easier to look out the window than turn to the woman in the apron behind the counter, whose discomfort with him was palpable from where he was sitting. In the window, he could catch her reflection, just a rough image of her, but he knew she was looking his way. He drank his coffee and picked at the sweet roll. Its taste matched his memory. But its sweetness no longer matched his mood.

The window reflection seemed to turn its back on him. He glanced back at her. She was wiping the counter, her back to him. She had dark-brown hair, with random streaks of gray running through it. Her hair was pulled back into a loose braid, some of the pieces slipping free. He wondered what that braid might feel like in his hand. She turned around and glanced at him. Caught. She raised her eyes up at his, as if to ask him what he was looking at. He smiled. She looked down and fussed with something he couldn't see. She was not exactly pretty, but yet, there was something compelling about her. Her eyes. The way her chest pulled at the apron. Something. Now he was the one who felt a bit uncomfortable, and he shifted in his chair and turned to look back out at the street. Henry was rarely at a loss for what to say, but at that moment, near this woman, he felt oddly silenced.

Henry finished his coffee and put the remainder of his sweet roll back into the bag. He brought the empty mug back to the counter, not wanting to leave it on the table.

"Thanks," he said. "That was good."

"Sure," the woman answered. "Anytime." She smiled quickly.

"Okay, see you next time," Henry replied, wanting to say more, not wanting to leave. He wanted to grab her hand, bring her around the counter, sit her down at the table near the window and ask her what the hell she was doing in a town like this, where she was from, and most importantly, what her name was. But he hesitated, and in that moment, she must have known, she must have sensed his indecision, and so she turned back to her busy work. And Henry turned and left, with the bells jangling.

Naomi Blue

Naomi saw the interest in this guy's eyes, but as he came up to the counter with his dishes, she also saw that he was young, too young. It had taken her some years to realize that thirty-nine was not twenty-nine. And while she sometimes appeared younger than she was, she wasn't interested in the life issues of people in their twenties. Some years are not worth reminiscing about. Nor are they worth regretting. The past was the past. Forgetting was the best strategy. In this guy's eyes, she saw those years she was glad to leave behind.

She also had seen that he had something to say, something he had been about to say; she could see it, sense it, feel it. She had quite knowingly taken away his chance.

Chapter Two

Naomi Blue

As Naomi walked home from the bakery that afternoon, she glanced at the people running late-afternoon errands. She figured some were really heading down to the bars for a quick drink before heading home. It sounded tempting, but it was the kind of thing Naomi wouldn't really do. No, she wouldn't go to a bar alone. And while she didn't think of herself as a loner, she probably looked like one, walking head down, watching the cracks in the sidewalk disappear under her feet. Naomi thought of herself as independent and confident. Her move to this town was an example of that, she believed. But she also believed that her independent behavior came from a fear of repeating her past—the particular kind of past where a series of relationships seem to have similarly unpleasant outcomes. She shook herself loose of these thoughts. Too late in the day to be so analytical. No good would come of it. Being self-reliant is okay, she thought. In fact, it's better than okay. Good. Yes, really good. The nagging feeling that undermined all this strength was the sense of isolation she had felt since moving into the widow's house. Reading the weekly paper had not made her feel a part of the community. Yet the simple pattern of her life, the job in the bakery, the quiet town, reading the paper, and just existing, felt enough for Naomi. At least that was what she told herself.

She altered her route home, despite the cold air that had moved in after the morning wind. She wanted to walk past Mikey's. *I'm not going in, of course,* she thought. *I'm not one for bars.* But still, the possibility existed that she just might go in if she walked by it. As she neared the bar, she felt queasy in her stomach. Naomi Blue did not go into bars. She felt out of place in them, not sure what to do with her legs—cross them, tuck them under the stool rungs. Or what to do with her hands— hold her drink, place them under the counter. Or where to look, how to tip, how to banter. How did she get to be this age and not learn to find comfort in a neighborhood bar? She glanced up at the front window as she passed. Posters advertising the upcoming high school play were lined up across the bottom. She could see shadowy images of people inside. A Budweiser sign flickered over the bar. Naomi kept on going.

Henry Alexander

Henry sat at the counter, leaning into his beer. He loved this place because, for the most part, nobody felt any boundaries. People sat next to him and talked. Or they didn't. Young women came in together and flirted, leaning forward to talk to him, giving him glimpses down their shirts, which he couldn't avoid, didn't even try to avoid, and nor did they expect him to. Men in Carhartt overalls came in and talked about the weather, their thick ruddy hands wrapped around their steins of beer. He felt a part of something. He felt part of the town in a way he hadn't felt growing up here. But this early fall afternoon, his mood was low, and he wasn't sure he was a part of anything. Perhaps Mikey's wasn't the best way to become a part of Copper Prairie again.

He was aware that he was moping, but so what, he thought. He could mope. Just when he was feeling particularly self-indulgent and thinking about getting another beer, he saw her—the bakery girl. She was walking right down the sidewalk, head down, as if trying not to step on the cracks in the concrete. At first, he wasn't sure it was the girl, but the pink Ida's Bakery shirt made him certain. The fact that her shirt was tight and the evening was cool drew his attention, though it wasn't the only attraction. There was something about how she had kept her distance, how she avoided talking with him earlier in the day. It was—it was just something. She glanced up at him—right at him—but didn't smile, didn't show recognition, didn't wave. She blinked, looked back down, and was gone. He was tempted to leave his beer and go after her, follow her down the street, walk with her, talk with her, take her home, and see what might happen. But, once again, he hesitated just long enough to know that it was already too late. He leaned his elbows on the counter and looked at the golden foam around the side of the glass.

IDA MINSKY

IDA MINSKY LOOKED AROUND the bakery before shutting the lights. The girl did her job well, yes, she did. The counters were flour free, the floor swept and mopped, the open sign turned around, the cafe chairs upside down on the tables, the lights in the bakery display off, and the door locked. Ida was, however, out of pecans, an ingredient she needed for tomorrow morning. Her regular delivery was a few days out, so she decided to walk over to Robinson's Grocery on Main Street. *Ach*, she thought, *that man will charge me too much for the nuts, but what's my choice, not to bake pecan rings?* Ida kept to a schedule, and tomorrow required pecans. You can't use walnuts when you need pecans. No, that won't do. She imagined the pecans around the top of the rings, glazed in honey and stickiness. She hung her apron on a hook and pulled her old green wool coat from the hook near the back door. Robinson's it was.

She felt the bite of autumn this evening as she walked down the street. If you watched Ida Minsky walk down the street, you would notice a distinct unevenness in her gait, the sense that one leg was perhaps longer than the other. In fact, it was. Her steps were uneven, a staccato step on the right leg, back over to the left. Nobody asked her why this was, but it was many years ago, when she was only five, that polio had found its way into her body, despite her mother's warnings and superstitious garlands of garlic around her neck. The doctors said she might never walk again. But with braces on her legs for two years, she had hobbled to grade school. The kids teased her only in the beginning. As she grew older, it was the kind of thing no one noticed. And if they did, they didn't ask questions. She had once tried wearing a shoe on her right side that was higher, a lift built into the sole, but there was something about such vanity that made Ida feel like a fraud. So she wore regular shoes, comfortable shoes, and kept on walking in her rocking way. She paid no mind. Despite an ache in her knees and hips, she kept going. Perhaps if she lost a few pounds it would be easier on her joints. At this age, it didn't matter how she looked. But the ache, the stiffness, this is what made her feel the years. Maybe she would eat less cake.

Rooster Robinson was not at the front register when she came into the store. A boy was busy changing the register tape and ignored her entry. She felt relief that Rooster wasn't there. He would be too interested in what she was buying and was a grouchy old man worth avoiding. *Always like he's doing me a favor having the store open, doing me a favor by having bananas or apples. What's wrong with that man. I do him a favor by shopping here. He should be glad I buy anything.* Ida went down the baking goods aisle. Nuts were on the bottom shelf. *It figures, my poor joints.* She bent over to grab four of the largest bags of pecans. It was all she could do not to groan as she stood up. She decided to see what

Rooster had in the deli and meat section that would make a healthy supper. By the time she saw Rooster it was too late to turn around.

"Hello, Mrs. Minsky, how are you this evening, huh?"

"I'm fine, Mr. Robinson, just fine."

"What's that? Nuts you got?"

She wished he hadn't noticed. She wanted her purchases to be private. She hid her irritation. And she was quite irritated to be paying his prices.

"Pecans. For tomorrow."

"Ah . . ."

Ida felt she'd gotten off easy, that Rooster was being a bit less ornery than usual. She eyed the meat counter.

"Hungry too, Mrs. Minsky?"

"Yes, well, could I have a pound of ground beef, if you would?"

Rooster Robinson pulled off a sheet of waxed butcher paper and scooped out the meat onto it, weighed it, wrapped it up, and marked a price in a black grease pencil.

"Here you go," he said, handing it over the counter to Ida.

"Thank you."

"My pleasure. So, what are you making with those pecans anyway?"

"Pecan rings, for Tuesday. Every Tuesday I bake them. You wouldn't know that, would you?"

"Hmph."

Ida raised an eyebrow at him and turned to walk down the aisle to the register. She felt his eyes on her back and was uncharacteristically self-conscious of her uneven walk. She made an effort to straighten herself and nearly lost her balance, leaning into the display on the end of the aisle to keep upright. Unfortunately, the boy who had stacked the new line of healthy low-sodium soups had had too much fun making a pyramid, and the slightest touch of Ida's hand caused the cans to tumble, not slowly, but all at once, a river of cans cascading to the floor. The cans fell loudly, rolling around the front of the store in all directions.

Ida reddened from her neck upward, offering up a quick prayer of thanks that she hadn't gone down with the soup. But other than that, not thankful for much. Rooster Robinson, a man only a few inches taller than Ida herself but looming large in his anger, came rushing down the aisle, muttering dark words she couldn't distinguish.

"I'm sorry!" she exclaimed.

"Don't fall, Mrs. Minsky. Stay put for one moment. Please don't move."

Rooster Robinson and the boy from the checkout register began corralling the soup cans, which had finally stopped rolling. She waited where she was, the men crawling around for the cans.

It was another ten minutes before she had paid for her meat and her pecans and heard the grocery store door close behind her.

Ida walked back to the bakery as quickly as she could, feeling the embarrassment of the debacle in Robinson's Grocery still on her back. She laid the bags of pecans on the counter and made her way upstairs with the meat. She'd lost her appetite. *That man*, she thought, *is rude*. And why would anyone stack cans like that in a store where people could bump into them? So inconvenient. So dangerous. She could have been hurt. That Rooster Robinson. Her embarrassment did not stem from her own clumsiness, but rather from the sense that Rooster had clearly enjoyed the scene. This only made her angrier. She sat in her chair in front of the window, watching over town until the street lamps came on.

Naomi Blue

THE EVENING FREIGHT CAME right on time that night, 10:24 p.m. The rumblings and vibration were nearly comforting. The world was orderly and on time. But what Naomi didn't know was that this was not an ordinary night. Nervous and disoriented, terrified of the intensity of the freight cars, feeling the weight of the train on the tracks right up through her paws, was a dog. She was a mixed breed, a large dog of uncertain parentage. Uncertain as far as anyone in the state of Minnesota was concerned. She had followed the tracks for almost a week, finding food where she could find it, where children had dropped treats in their sandboxes, in the alleys behind grocery marts, around bird feeders, and once a train engineer had tossed her the crust of a salami sandwich. She was hungry and in need of a good brushing. Burs were stuck in the fur on her back and on her hind legs. The nights were getting cold, and she was weary. She stopped finally, crawling into a ball of fur between two peony shrubs against the gray house near the tracks.

Naomi woke to the surprising sound of whimpering outside her window, a sound more like the whining cry of a child who wanted to stay up late than of a hungry dog. She tossed on a sweatshirt and ran downstairs, slowly opening the back door. The dog was sitting there, cautiously. It stopped its crying and lifted one paw, as if to shake, but not exactly. A tentative gesture. Naomi knelt on the top step, unsure. "Where did you come from?" The dog took a step closer. "Are you friendly?" The dog sat down again. "You look like a sweet dog." The dog lifted its paw again. Naomi Blue reached over to the dog, let it sniff her hand, and then touched it behind the ear. The dog's eyes squinted in pleasure. "I bet you're thirsty, aren't you." Naomi scooted back into the house, grabbed a bowl and filled it with water. It looked up at her briefly, and then began to lap at the water. Naomi watched.

The dog had no collar, no tags. And, thought Naomi, *no name*. She picked off the burs that had embedded themselves in her fur, speaking calmly. Feeling some comfort in the dog's demeanor, Naomi opened the back door and said, "C'mon, pup."

The dog only hesitated for a moment and then trotted up the steps. Once settled with more water and also a bowl of Cheerios that were the closest thing Naomi had to dog food, Naomi contemplated her options. She could see if anyone had lost the dog. But if no one claimed the dog, she could keep it. She didn't know much about dogs, but this one seemed trained and sweet. Good enough. The dog needed a name. The dog had curled up on a braided rug in the kitchen, eyes closed. When Naomi moved, the dog opened its eyes, watching her, keeping track of her. Beatrix. She was officially named.

She made a call to the police station to see if anyone had lost a dog. No one had, but she found out that dogs needed license tags and that would cost her twenty dollars. "Twenty dollars?" she had asked. "How can that be?"

Officer Millerton explained, "License fees, m'am, for the police department. Perhaps you didn't know that it's mostly volunteer."

"No," Naomi responded. "I didn't know that."

"Well, those fees pay for the police force's animal control pickup truck that does double duty in town. Yup, double duty. Not only does it go out on calls for wayward dogs, squirrels in attics, and the like, but it also patrols our streets for road kills. Cleans up the streets. Not a job too many officers enjoy, but someone has to do it, and with gloves and a mask, it's not too bad. Easiest in winter. Doesn't smell so bad."

"Okay," Naomi said to the officer. "I get it." Naomi laughed and said she'd be down to pick up the forms soon. *Hopefully when a less talkative officer is on duty*, she thought as she hung up the phone.

Beatrix also needed a collar and a leash. Maybe even a couple of dog bowls, since letting her use two of the four cereal bowls seemed extravagant, if not disgusting. Naomi Blue had only once before had a dog, and he hadn't lasted long. The dog had come from a litter of pups found along the shore of a lake by an older couple walking off their Thanksgiving dinner, the wind pulling at their hoods. But a whimpering sound had penetrated their conversation, and they'd found six small, still sweet-smelling puppies crying in the bushes. The couple had gathered them up in their coats and brought them to the local animal shelter. Meanwhile, Naomi had been a regular visitor to the shelter, stopping in to see the dogs, although not ever intending to take one home. She knew little about dogs. She harbored a certain degree of fear towards them, having been nipped on the side of her nose by a tan cocker spaniel when she was eleven at her friend Sarah's house. So taking a dog home was not really her intention. But still, she had picked up one of the beach puppies and held it until she got home. The puppy tore apart her cushions, ate her shoelaces, and one day dragged a roll of toilet paper throughout her apartment. When he reached seventy-five pounds in a matter of months, the destruction increased exponentially. Ashamed, she'd brought the dog back to the shelter. And now Beatrix.

Chapter Three

Henry Alexander

DECIDING TO RUN FOR ELDERMAN was not exactly a decision, Henry admitted to himself. It was more like a revelation. Sitting in the bar that night, sitting way too long by the window, he was feeling both self-pitying and introspective. A woman sat down beside him.

"I know you, don't I?"

Thinking that it sounded like a come-on line, he turned to look at her. Something vaguely familiar, but he couldn't place her.

"I don't know. Do you?"

"Sure, you're Hank Alexander, right?"

"No one calls me Hank anymore. But yeah, that's me."

"We went to high school together. At Central."

Henry looked over at her as she took a large swallow of beer.

"I don't remember your name."

"Millie Bing. Actually I wasn't Bing then. I was Johnson. Margaret Rose Johnson according to the yearbook. Ring a bell?"

"I think so. Yeah, Millie Johnson." Henry wasn't sure about this, wasn't sure he remembered her at all, but it was some time ago, and he'd been gone for a while, and it was more polite to remember her than not.

"Weren't you really involved with that environmental club or something like that?" she asked.

"Yeah, we called ourselves the POPs. Protecting Our Prairie. We had these goofy green-and-white shirts that we wore all the time. But we did cool stuff. It was a good club."

"Right," Millie replied, sounding doubtful. "I was on the pep squad. One of those girls who didn't make the cheerleading team, couldn't quite do those moves, so was on the pep squad. We went to all the games. You didn't play any sports, did you?"

"Nope. I wasn't into sports at all, unless you count frisbee."

They talked over another drink, playing the standard game of life catch-up that Henry didn't much care for.

"So you're married?" he asked.

"Divorced actually. But I kind of liked the name Bing. Bing like the cherries." She smiled.

"Ah."

"What about you? You married?" she asked casually, as if she didn't really care, but he was certain she did.

"Nope, never married. Still finding my way."

They drank their beers quietly, as Henry returned to his brooding mood. Millie's interest made him cautious.

"So why are you back in Copper Prairie? Does your family still live here?" she asked.

"No, my folks retired to Arizona. I came back because, well, because I needed out of the Cities, and this was home, I guess."

Henry wasn't even sure about this. When things soured in Minneapolis with his girlfriend and he had to move out quickly, he had nowhere to go. Moving in with his parents was not an option, even less of an option because they were now out west. Copper Prairie seemed the only choice, a refuge, a last resort. So far, the town had disappointed him with its ordinances, its lack of environmental concern, and in a general sense, its small-town qualities. But coming back had seemed important. Inevitable even.

"Sometimes coming back is coming home. Sometimes it's not," Millie remarked.

"I'm just frustrated by this town sometimes," he said.

"So do something about it," she said, downing the remainder of her beer.

He looked at her curiously but didn't say anything in response. But he did begin to think. His sudden quiet might have given her the impression that he wasn't interested in the conversation anymore, and perhaps that he wasn't interested in her anymore. Indeed, Henry was not interested in her, and hadn't been in the first place. She seemed to need something, and it wasn't something he was interested in giving.

Saying something about it getting late, and nice to see her again after all this time, maybe see her there again sometime, he'd tipped the bartender and spun around on his stool.

He would do something. He would run for office. At least it would be something to do.

Naomi Blue

Naomi soon found that Beatrix was an attention hound of sorts. People stopped to comment. "What kind of dog is she?" "Wow, what a cute dog." "Can I pet her?" It had been a couple of weeks since she'd reported finding the dog to the nearest pet store, vet, and police department. No one had reported a missing dog so far. Naomi felt comfortable attaching the red collar and tags that identified her as Beatrix. But she didn't quite feel comfortable in actually claiming the dog as her own. She didn't want to grow attached to her, and then have a family knock on the door, happy to see their missing dog. For her part, Beatrix seemed to be content to follow Naomi around the house, lying on the nearest area rug to watch her closely, until she relaxed securely into sleep. While Naomi went to work, Beatrix slept on her bed, leaving traces of her dark fur on the blanket. No shoes were destroyed, no pillows eaten. After a few nights of Beatrix sleeping on the bed, alternately snoring and running in her sleep, Naomi Blue relegated the dog to a cushiony bed on the floor.

The next Friday morning began with the sound of whimpers. Naomi thought perhaps her alarm hadn't gone off at first, but soon realized that it was the dog. She'd worked long hours at the bakery. She tried ignoring the sound of the dog but worried that her selfishness would turn into a clean-up job. Beatrix put her nose against Naomi's cheek.

"Okay, okay. You sure do have a cold nose."

The dog's tail began to wag—or rather, her whole back end swayed in delight as Naomi got out of bed, put her feet into a pair of wool socks, and went downstairs. The dog bounded ahead, her tail whacking anything nearby. She laughed at the energy that this animal had brought into the house. She grabbed the paper from where it had miraculously landed on the front porch. Must have been a good morning for the delivery kid, she thought.

The front-page article was about the residents who had filed for the three open elderman seats on the city governing council. The filing deadline had passed three days ago with five people filing. Naomi thought it peculiar that the town of Copper Prairie elected eldermen rather than city councilmen or commissioners or just aldermen. City elders. Just the word elderman conjured up images in her mind of grizzly older bearded men sitting on log benches around a fire in the open prairie deciding which route the wagon train should take. She scanned the photos of the candidates, and was startled to realize that she recognized one. It was the guy from the bakery. Henry Morgan Alexander. *What a pretentious name*, Naomi thought. Henry Morgan Alexander, resident of Copper Prairie, single, age twenty-nine. Too young to be an elderman, she laughed to herself. This was crazy. Running for office? Henry? He smiled out from the paper. She tore the article out to save, and used one of the five fruit refrigerator magnets to post it on the refrigerator.

Despite the collar on Beatrix's neck, Naomi felt her ownership of the dog to be more of a mutual agreement between animal and woman. The dog had found her. She had taken the dog in. But she felt it was only fair to let her out back without being tied up, even without a fenced yard. If Beatrix were to follow the tracks out of town, then so be it. Naomi Blue let the dog out the back door to sniff and do her business in the small backyard. Eventually, Beatrix would end up back on the step, lying in the sun, or sitting alertly watching for rabbits.

Naomi made a cup of coffee and looked out the back screen door to see if Beatrix was waiting to come in or stretched out on the step, her paws hanging over the edge. No Beatrix. She opened the door, gently maneuvering the full cup of coffee so that the slamming of the screen door wouldn't knock her arm. There she was. Despite Naomi Blue's noble thoughts of their ownership relationship, she did not want the dog to run off or find another home. She wanted to be chosen by the dog, she liked being wanted. She stepped out to the yard to see what Beatrix was doing. The dog was sniffing the shed in the back corner of the yard.

"Beatrix, what's there? A rabbit?" Beatrix barely lifted her nose from the weeds, ignoring her, intent on whatever scent she had grabbed on to. Beatrix went around to the back of the shed, eventually emerging around the front.

"Beatrix!"

The dog trotted over to where Naomi was sitting on the back step, her coffee mug steaming beside her. Burs were caught up in Beatrix's fur, embedded in knotted tangled balls behind her collar. She sat patiently while Naomi pulled them out, sticky burs that caught onto Naomi's own clothes as she released them from the fur.

"What was so interesting over there, huh, girl?" Together they walked back towards the shed, the dog's tail wagging fiercely.

Naomi Blue had not given the shed any real attention, having not located the key to the padlock, which lay rusted against the hasp. Maybe there was a lawnmower in there, Naomi thought. Or a rake, or shovel, or something useful. But Naomi was not really interested in yard work, and the effort of finding a way into this dilapidated shack was not worth the possibility of chores ahead of her if she found yard tools.

"Come on, Beatrix, forget the shack. Another day."

Chapter Four

Ida Minsky

IDA DIDN'T SLEEP WELL at all that night. Standing on Carriage Street looking up at the window, a passerby would have seen her sitting there for a long time and then eventually, would have seen the curtain pulled across the window and the light extinguished. Ida went to sleep early, much earlier than the rest of the town. She used to laugh to herself that her bedtime was the same as the third-grade school children. Her mornings began earlier than theirs though. While she rarely remembered her dreams, she might wake with the vague awareness that she had been with someone or had done something. She had a few dreams that seemed to repeat with variations. Usually, they were of baking and forgetting to take things out of the oven. Dreams where cakes were blackened, or loaves of bread started the oven on fire, or worse, where smoke streamed out of the bakery up to her apartment.

She awoke suddenly at three o'clock in the morning, absolutely awake, dreaming of the smell of smoke. She got up, pulled her robe around her, tied it snugly at the waist, slid her feet into her slippers, and padded downstairs slowly, so as not to trip. She knew there was no chance something was in the oven, but the dream's feeling of reality forced her to be sure. She superstitiously believed that dreams had some truth to them. The hall light lit up the back of the bakery. Nothing was on. Nothing was baking.

There was no smoke, no smell of gas, nothing. *What's wrong with me*, Ida chastised herself, *I'm worrying too much.*

She went slowly, very slowly back up the stairs and sat heavily on the bed. She loved the feel of her crisp white sheets and the weight of her blankets, three of them actually, upon her body. She closed her eyes. (Relax, Ida. One more hour and then you can get up.) She drifted into that state of sleep closer to awake than dreams. Rooster Robinson floated through her mind. He was watching her walk down the street, watching her and smiling. Mocking? Admiring? Laughing?

Ida's morning began in the dark, as it always did. She felt sluggish and not ready to start the day's baking. Yet as she began working, her spirits lifted. She loved the keen smell of yeast, both when it was proofing and when it had been mixed into a smooth elastic dough set to rise. The smell of yeast was inextricably linked to the scent of childhood, of flour on a marble slab, kneeling on a stool beside her mother whose floral apron barely reached around to tie in the back. The smell of yeast was the essence of mother. While various batches of dough were rising, she chopped pecans, raisins, prepared a series of pans, and created an organized mess of flour, white sugar, brown sugar, baking powder, and other ingredients. Her mood flourished in the kitchen. The feeling of creating something, of making something where nothing existed before, of seeing the neat beauty of the ring cakes, the pecans sprinkled carefully yet randomly on top—these were the things that defined her. Creating delicately risen rolls, round and smooth on top, a hint of flour along the bottom, ah, thought Ida, that was beautiful. The smells of the bakery were a sort of ecstasy for her. The uneasiness of her night had passed as she awaited the morning arrival of the girl who would wait on the customers and talk to the customers, while she baked in the back.

The girl was never early, that much Ida knew. But today she came in precisely at seven, as if she had waited for the hour hand to click into place at the seven before pushing open the door.

"Good morning, Mrs. Minsky," Naomi said as she closed the door behind her. "How are you?"

"Yah, good morning, Naomi. Good morning."

"It smells unbelievable in here today. Better than ever. I just love coming in that door and breathing in."

Ida Minsky felt flattered and looked closely at the girl to see if her face looked as genuine as her voice sounded. She herself felt that kind of joy in the bakery, but the girl? Naomi was tying her apron around her waist and seemed startled when she looked up at Ida staring at her.

"What, Mrs. Minsky? What's wrong?"

"Nothing. I'm glad you like being here. It is good. It is also good to enjoy the smell more than the taste, or you will get fat like me."

"Too late, I think," said Naomi, patting her hips. "Too late."

Ida smiled and went back to the floured counter to work. Naomi washed her hands and got ready to wait on customers. The day had begun.

Naomi Blue

Naomi had actually been leaving the house early that day and might even have been ten minutes early to work if she hadn't turned around a block from home to find something to wear over the t-shirt. There was a frost in the air, and she figured it was time to find something warm to wear. She pulled open the closet door and pushed back the hangers. There wasn't much to choose from. An old sweatshirt hung on a hook, royal blue, a sweatshirt she'd had for more years than anything else in her closet. White letters spelled out Buffalo in an arc across her chest. Her cousin had gone to the New York State University in Buffalo and had sent it to her so long ago she couldn't remember exactly where she'd been living at the time. She'd opened the package and wondered why he had sent her an extra large, offended at the implication, but in the end, had worn it anyhow. She was invisible beneath it. Her cousin was living somewhere in New Hampshire now, although Naomi had lost track of him after he returned from a yearlong trek through Europe. She hadn't lost track of the sweatshirt, however, and she pulled it over her head and said goodbye to Beatrix again and left for the bakery. She was relieved not to be late; she didn't want to lose this job. Not only did it give her a paycheck, but it also gave her day meaning, a schedule, a place to go, and often, something delicious to eat.

Today was one of those days. Ida's pecan rings were Naomi's favorite. The cinnamon rolls may have a historical reputation, but the pecan rings were Naomi's favorite. In the morning quiet, before the customers came in, she was able to enjoy the cake and a cup of fresh coffee. The day was good so far.

The door opened a bit later and a man came in. He was a short stocky man with a dark scowl across his forehead that Naomi figured was permanent on his face.

"Hello, can I help you?" she greeted him.

"Uh, yes. Let me look first."

He was vaguely familiar to Naomi. She knew she'd seen him somewhere before, and thought if he was there long enough, she might place him.

"Do you sell that pecan thing by the slice, miss?"

"Yes, we do. Would you like a piece?" Naomi was aware that Ida Minsky was quiet in the back, not moving about anymore. She knew Ida Minsky was listening. Why did that woman have to mistrust her so? Why did she think she'd be rude to customers? In her annoyance, Naomi heaped on the sweetness.

"Would you like some coffee too, sir?"

"Uh, no, thank you. But could you give me that one—that bigger slice—yeah, that one. It looks good."

"For here or to go?"

"To go."

Naomi slid the slice into a waxed paper bag.

"Anything else?"

"That's all, miss. Thank you."

Naomi rang him up and thanked him. He opened the door and then awkwardly, half out the door into the cold, turned back towards Naomi.

"Tell Mrs. Minsky that I came for her pecan cake. Tell her Roger Robinson came by." And he was gone before Naomi could reply that Mrs. Minsky was just five feet away.

She turned around. "Mrs. Minsky?"

Ida stood there, hands on her hips, looking past Naomi, at the door. Naomi couldn't tell if the flush on her face was from the heat of the ovens, anger or embarrassment. Ida shook her head slowly and went back to her work. Naomi knew not to say anything more, but wondered what that was all about. Roger Robinson? Rooster Robinson from the grocery store. Much nicer than his reputation, she mused.

IDA MINSKY

WHAT WAS THE MEANING OF THAT DISPLAY? Ida fumed in front of the ovens, her back to the girl. She had recognized his gravelly voice from the moment he spoke to Naomi. She had frozen in the back, not wanting to make any noise, not wanting to come forward. He was a dark, unpleasant man, Ida thought, and she had intended to steer clear of the grocery store for as long as possible, even if it meant eating her pantry full of bad-weather emergency canned goods. She would do that, yes she would, eat all her cream of mushroom soups and canned corn rather than face Rooster Robinson again soon. Let him forget about that episode in his store. She hoped he would forget about it quickly.

What did that man want with her anyway, she wondered. Ordering a slice of her pecan ring—what was that all about? Maybe he just wanted to see how his damn pecans tasted in my cake. Yes, maybe he just wanted to take some credit.

There was no way that Ida Minsky would admit to herself the kindness that his voice had held, the eagerness with which he ordered the cake, and the sincerity in asking after her. There were some things she was simply not willing to admit, though she was aware of the growing sense of pleasure she felt throughout the rest of the day.

Chapter Five

Naomi Blue

Naomi's days off came infrequently because Ida Minsky didn't have other employees and wanted her there any time the bakery was open. They had agreed that Naomi would simply ask for a day off when she wanted one. When she did, Ida would put her floured hands on her hips, pause, and then say yes. Naomi knew that it was not given to her happily. This also meant that Naomi felt a certain amount of guilt sleeping late, knowing that Ida was alone in the bakery. But she shed that guilt quickly as she stretched back out in her bed after letting the dog out, the open shades in her room letting in the rather dim light of the fall morning. Frost edged her old leaky windows.

Eventually Naomi threw on a pair of jeans and a speckled gray cable knit cardigan. A day to walk the dog, she thought. Beatrix didn't get the attention she knew the animal deserved. The inactivity was surely the cause of the extra girth growing around the dog's middle. At least her collar still fit, although she had moved the notch over once so far.

It was early enough in the day that most of the stores were closed, and there were traces of last night's happenings on the sidewalks, particularly in front of the Ringworm where cigarette butts were pressed into the concrete. Beatrix sniffed the ground intensely as they walked through town, looking for bits of food that may have fallen from a child's hand. Towards the end of town was a QuikStop gas station. Being the only gas station in town meant that the prices stayed higher than they might have been otherwise, yet business remained steady. Naomi was glancing at the large sign to see what the price of a gallon had gotten up to when a pickup truck began to back up. A split second later she saw a young woman on the ground. The truck stopped, half backed up. The woman turned on her side and hesitated before trying to lean on an elbow. Before Naomi could reach her, she was sitting.

"Are you okay?" Naomi exclaimed. Beatrix pulled on the leash, excited over the short run.

"What happened?" the woman said after struggling to stand up. She looked at Naomi and then at the truck. A man came out from behind the wheel, as a woman came out of the passenger side.

"Are you okay?" he asked.

"What happened?" the woman asked again. "You hit me."

"No, I don't think so," said the man.

"You walked into the car," said the woman from the truck. "You walked into us."

Naomi listened. Had she seen the truck hit the woman? What had happened? Had the woman walked into the truck? Was that possible? Could that have happened? No way.

"I think you ought to sit down," Naomi said, taking her elbow. "I'm Naomi. I don't think you ought to have gotten up. But come, sit here on the bench."

The woman let Naomi lead her to the bench outside the gas station store. It smelled foul, like old urine, and Naomi sat down uneasily. But the woman should not be moving around.

"What's your name?"

"My name? I'm Millie. What's yours?"

"I'm Naomi. Naomi Blue. I'm going to call the police."

Naomi realized that the couple from the truck were standing a few yards away watching, their truck still at an angle half out of the parking place.

"She walked into us, you know," the woman from the truck said. Looking at Millie directly she said, "It was your fault, you walked into us."

"Shut up, honey. Be quiet. Go back to the truck." The man came over to them on the bench.

"What can I do?" he asked.

"Stick around," Naomi said. "I'm calling the police."

But there was no need to call the police since Copper Prairie's police force already knew.

Dan Millerton had a small Cape Cod house at the edge of town. Being a police officer was all he'd ever wanted to do. From the time he was four, he knew he wanted to wear the blue uniform, shirt tucked in, dark leather belt, black shoes, and of course, the badge. Every Halloween he was a policeman, until he got too old to wear a costume, and then he went around the neighborhoods with the other boys carrying pillowcases to haul candy, but it was never the same when he couldn't wear the costume. There wasn't a teacher or student at Copper Prairie Central School who was surprised when Dan Millerton became a police officer. It wasn't about the power of the job, or even about being able to carry a gun. It was about the tidiness and look of the uniform itself. He could never have been an undercover police officer—he needed that uniform. Office Millerton kept his blond hair buzzed military short, and his shoes shined to a reflection.

Office Millerton's arrival at the gas station was not delayed by waiting for a phone call, or even by the time it would take to get there. Rather, it was delayed by the time it took him to put his coffee mug in the sink, fill it with water, race back to his room, take his neatly hung uniform from his closet, get dressed, check himself in the mirror, run his hand through his hair and open the front door.

Naomi was relieved to see the police officer walking towards them. She didn't like the woman from the truck too much, loudly denying any responsibility, blaming Millie. But Naomi wasn't entirely sure what had happened. She was only sure of two things— the price of gas and that a woman had been lying on the ground. For her part, Millie did not seem quite aware of what was going on. She was holding her shoulder and rubbing it. Her pants were dirty, and the wet stain that was spreading on her knee was probably blood.

"What's your name again?" Millie asked Naomi.

"Naomi. You'll be okay. Just sit tight."

Office Millerton walked up to the bench. Beatrix greeted him with a sniff of his feet and then lifting her nose up towards the officer's hands. Naomi took a quick glance at his nametag, thought his name looked familiar, and introduced herself, explaining what she knew. Officer Millerton took charge quickly, did a brief evaluation of Millie and called for the Copper Prarie Volunteer Ambulance Squad. Within moments of their arrival, they had Millie in a neck brace. Office Millerton took the couple off to the side to interview them. Naomi ran inside the gas station and jotted her name and phone number down on a scrap of paper. Before they took Millie away, she slipped the paper into her pocket. "Millie, let me know how it goes. Call me when you get home."

Millie looked up at Naomi, her head held straight, eyes forward. She blinked.

Henry Alexander

Filing for city elderman had not been too hard. All it took was a simple form completed while standing at the clerk's counter at city hall. The clerk had stamped it "received" and thanked him. She then handed him a small packet of information to read. He'd felt a fluttering in his gut on the way home, as if he had done something tremendous, noteworthy, something completely outside his realm. When the newspaper was delivered that listed the candidates' names, he was certain he had done something unlike anything he'd done before. His parents would probably ask him why, what had possessed him to run for city elder. Why, he was hardly a man, his mother would say, how could he be an elder. He knew they would question his credentials. So he kept this detail of his life from their twice-monthly Sunday phone calls. Mostly they were interested in their own peers who had not left Copper Prairie. Sometime he clipped out articles from the *Copper Press* to send them.

Henry sat down on the futon that doubled as couch and bed in his small apartment at the top floor of a house on Oak Street. Now that a week had passed since he'd filed, he figured it was time to find out what being a city elder meant exactly. The packet was partly a listing of state election law regulating campaign fundraising and spending, as well as local city government ordinances and policies. "Roles of the City Elderman" was the title of the first document he decided to read. First item on the list was to be responsive to the needs of the residents of Copper Prairie.

How was he going to actually get himself elected, Henry wondered. What would that take? In a town of 15,000, it wouldn't be too hard to knock on doors and introduce himself, would it? He could make lawn signs maybe. He realized he didn't know the first thing about running for office. Not the first thing. But since moving back to Copper Prairie, he had been living off his savings rather than working so he would have the time to learn. Maybe a slogan is what he needed, a slogan or platform to get his candidacy rolling. Or something that he believed in. The only problem was, he wasn't sure what that was. He decided that listening to "the people" would be a good place to start, hearing what mattered to them. Maybe this weekend he could listen to people at the Ringworm.

Naomi Blue

Naomi Blue was shaken. Seeing the woman laying on the ground and watching the ambulance cart her away were all it took for Naomi to reach into the freezer and grab the pint of ice cream. Buying smaller-sized containers was supposed to curb her consumption of her favorite food.

Typically, she divided the pint into three nights. But it was afternoon, it was a full pint, and her self-control seemed at a low point. She stood at the kitchen counter, looking out the back window, and began eating. She imagined herself in the parking lot knocked onto the concrete. Who would care if she'd been the one hurt? Who would know if she was in the hospital? Who would miss her? Naomi suddenly felt desperately alone and began to choke up with tears. That'll keep me from eating ice cream, she coughed. Beatrix, ever aware of Naomi's movements, came to see what the noise was. Perhaps the ice cream tempted her as well. Neither interested her, and she returned to her bed in the living room.

It was one of those times Naomi missed her mother who lived a continent away. She missed her mother in the childlike way that grown women miss their mothers. She missed the concept of mother she still held onto, the image of the woman who had tucked her in when she was a little girl, who had read her stories, put her socks on her feet, tied her shoes. That mother was long gone. That image of mother should be long gone, Naomi suspected, but the ache of it persisted.

Soon after her father had died, Naomi began to call her mother by her first name, Dora. She couldn't remember why that started, when she was no longer "mom" but now this woman, Dora. After a brief time grieving, Dora had fallen in love with a man nine years younger than herself. Ronald was a man unlike her father in nearly every way. And Ronald liked to fish. It was more than simply liking fishing; it was a passion for fishing. He would troll the ocean with gigantic fishing rods, hoping for the Big One. Ronald was also content with a pair of binoculars and a reclining chair so he could watch the birdfeeder in the backyard. He was a vegetarian, and the concoctions that her mother and Ronald created in the kitchen were full of beans, grains, and unrecognizable other ingredients. There was often a soy composite meant to resemble and replace meat. Her father's mainstay had been steak and potatoes—skip the green beans—every night of the week. Her father had played basketball and tennis until his knees and elbows gave out. Then he became famous for watching one sporting event after another on television all weekend long.

Dora's life had begun again, just the way Naomi thought it should after the death of a spouse. But so completely had her mother begun again, it was as if she was a new person and Naomi was no longer related to her. Ronald called her Dorrie, despite her mother's insistence throughout her earlier life that she only be called Dora. She in turn called him Ronnie. Dorrie and Ronnie retired to a small enclave of other American retirees in Costa Rica, a crazy hour's drive from San Jose. It was a beautiful small house, with decorative but impressive iron bars on the windows, not far from the Pacific Ocean. Dorrie and Ronnie were still taking Spanish lessons, four years after they'd moved south.

Naomi had visited them twice, the first time feeling trapped in her mother's new life and seeing very little of the country. Deep-sea fishing was one of the featured activities of the visit. Naomi had gamely gone with Ronald, not realizing that the swells on the ocean—even on a calm day—could make her seasick. She'd done pretty well controlling her stomach until Ronald's bait bucket had overturned on her feet. The pieces of fish, bloody guts, and slime had slipped between her toes, and she'd lost her balance and gone down in the mess. She promptly added to it. It was not a memory to revisit. On the second trip south, she'd hired a guide and had traveled throughout the country, finding it beautiful and haunting with its cloud forests, volcanoes, monkeys, and birds.

Costa Rica was far away. It was an international phone call away. There were no nonstop flights from Minnesota. And Naomi had taken French, not Spanish, in high school. Her mother was gone. And this woman Dorrie lived in Latin America.

IDA MINSKY

IDA MINSKY WASN'T DOING VERY WELL. Her nights continued to be restless on a good night and sleepless on a bad one. She dreamed of being a little girl in Chicago, the apartment building with its long flights of steps to the fifth floor, where she lived with her parents, her two brothers and her sister. She and her sister Rose shared a full-sized bed in a tiny room, while her brothers each had their own in the adjoining room. Her parents slept on a foldout couch in the living room. Why the children had the bedrooms was not something they ever talked about in the family, or frankly even thought about. It was only when Ida reached her twenties that she realized the sacrifice her immigrant parents had regularly made for their children. Privacy came in the quick bits of time you had in the bathroom, when you could get it. Ida's dreams seemed too reminiscent of her past to be dreams and she wondered if these memories were coming back for some reason. Maybe as you neared death you remembered the details of your life starting with your childhood. She remembered the polished oak of the banister in the stairwell, the frosted glass on the top half of the front door, the apartment number 5B in cursive brass bolted to the right of the door. She remembered the girl Julianna, who lived at 2D, her breasts tremendous in fourth grade, so big they were impossible to hide, and how the boys teased her, painfully, when in a few short years they would admire them. Where was Julianna now, Ida wondered.

Her sister Rose had died of a stroke when she was just fifty-nine, too young, too young. Ida remembered the look in her eyes as she had lain in the hospital bed, her face drooping off balance, her body not cooperating. But her eyes had looked at Ida's, and they had shut when Ida stroked her hair back off her face. Rose knew what was happening as her body slowed down. Her breaths began to come many seconds apart, then minutes, and then not at all.

Ida had owned the bakery for ten years already and had locked the door for the two weeks she'd spent with her sister, and then the week after she had died. After her death, Ida went through Rose's belongings, taking the clothes that might fit her, although few things were big enough. She put all of Rose's papers and photos in a box to sort through at home. Rose's husband, Morris, had watched Ida through it all, letting her rummage, and talking very little. He'd taken her hand one day, in kindness, nothing more, and Ida had misunderstood and jerked it back, not understanding his need to touch her hand, the living sister's hand. He did not try that again, for which Ida was grateful. It was many months before she regretted her reaction. She missed Rose, and Morris was one of the connections to her.

Rose had had so much attention being the married sister. Ida had not married, and did not ponder why too often. She liked men in the same way that she liked her brothers, but did not see the need to have one with her on a daily basis. Not that she hadn't had her share of romance. That she had. But Ida wore the moniker of businesswoman, not old maid. As a young woman, she had worked early hours in the kitchen of a small diner on the edge of the warehouse district in Chicago learning how to prepare salads and fish, Greek food and Italian. It was varied and she loved the heat and fast-paced intensity in the kitchen. One restaurant wanted her to waitress because she was a woman, but dealing with the customers was not her strength, and a flurry of complaints sent her back to the kitchen for good. Ida would come home to her Slavic non-English speaking mother, kneading the dough for bread, working it smooth, the smell of dough rising all afternoon. Ida watched and learned how to make all the wonderful treats she now served in her own bakery.

Ida began to welcome these thoughts parading through her mind at night and spilling into the daytime. There was some comfort in her past. Some pride. Besides, there seemed to be no way to sleep any better than with the people of her past keeping her company.

Chapter Six

Henry Alexander

The band playing at the Ringworm on Saturday night was a local folk band, the Cold Tree Friends. They had a fervent following of fans that came any time they played within seventy-five miles. Henry's music taste was broad, though folk music was not his first choice for a Saturday night. But the bar filled up when they played, making the owners happy watching the alcohol flow. Given that Henry's mission tonight was to reach out to his fellow citizens, he thought he might be able to talk over folk singers better than an alternative rock band. He vowed to make his beer last as long as possible and to be social.

By the time he got there, the Cold Tree Friends were halfway through their first set. He ordered a beer and a plate of nachos and found himself a table near the back. He'd listen first and then socialize. It occurred to Henry that this might not be the right venue for campaigning. He leaned back in his chair and listened to the band. A table of women he didn't know sat near the front, a bottle of wine on the table, and Henry watched their heads dip closely together to talk between songs. They laughed, sharing some secret, about men, he imagined. As the music played and the beer smoothed his mood, he decided this was not a night for campaigning. It was a night of watching.

NAOMI BLUE

Naomi's idea of a Saturday night was to take a book, a glass of red wine, and five pieces of milk chocolate into the bathtub—her favorite indulgences. Beatrix's fear of the sound of running water kept her outside the bathroom door, her snout flat against her paws. Even though the tub was a bit too small for a good soak, if Naomi Blue bent her legs slightly it was good enough. As the water neared the top of the tub, she took off her robe and glanced in the mirror. For so long, she had been unaware of time on her face, age on her body. But now, at nearly forty, Naomi noticed changes. Although they had happened slowly, Naomi noticed them abruptly. The skin under her chin seemed softer, looser. Her hair was definitely grayer, and her laugh lines deeper. Naomi sighed. She had never before thought of the changes of aging as negative or positive. But recently, the feeling of time passing made her uneasy. Just as Naomi was about to step into the bath, the phone rang. Another person might have ignored it, but her phone rang so infrequently she found it impossible to ignore. She hesitated a few seconds and ran naked to her room to grab the phone.

"Hello?"

"Hi, is this Naomi?"

"Yes, this is Naomi."

"Uh, this is Millie. Millie Bing, the woman who was hit by the car the other day. Remember?"

"Yes! Millie. Hi. Are you okay?"

"Yeah, I'm okay. I had a concussion, a cut on my knee, and I've got black-and-blue marks on my whole right side, but not too bad, considering."

"Wow."

"It was more scary than anything, I guess. I'm lucky it wasn't worse. He might not have stopped."

"I'm glad you're okay. That was awful. I was really upset about the whole thing."

"I just wanted to thank you. I mean, thanks for stopping and staying with me. For everything."

"It was no big deal."

"Maybe, but not everyone would do it, so it is a big deal to me. Thanks."

"Sure. Maybe one day someone will do that for me!"

"Let's hope not . . . I mean, let's hope it doesn't happen. So, I was wondering, uh, can I thank you somehow? Do you want to go out for a drink?"

"That would be okay. Sure."

"Well, I know this is last minute and all, but there's a really good folk band at the Ringworm tonight, and, well, it might be fun."

Naomi Blue was not a spontaneous sort of person. She had not gone out since she moved to Copper Prairie, and it made her feel a little guilty to think that a bath sounded like more fun. That guilt made her accept the offer.

"Okay, what time?"

"Meet me there at 8:30?"

"Okay, see you there."

Naomi hung up and slipped into the hot water. There was time enough for this. She leaned back against the curved top of the tub, popped one piece of chocolate into her mouth and closed her eyes. Going out to the Ringworm didn't really sound like a good time; sitting in a bar just wasn't her idea of a fun thing to do. But the months without socializing at all were weighing on her. She had promised herself when she moved to Copper Prairie that part of her fresh start would be to be more social and get involved with people, start to trust people. So far, she had made a list full of excuses as to why this wasn't happening. Too busy working, too busy with the house, and now too busy with the dog. Naomi wasn't fooling herself. Social inertia had taken over.

As she dressed, Naomi realized that she knew nothing at all about this woman, Millie. What would they talk about? Naomi felt an emptiness of life. Was there anything in her life to make her sound interesting? Would she be a lousy conversationalist? She reminded herself that this wasn't a date—it was a thank-you glass of wine from a stranger. Who cared if she were boring?

Naomi Blue walked over to the Ringworm. She could hear music before she even got to the front door. And there was Millie, walking towards her.

"Hey, Naomi, hi," Millie greeted her, her shoulders hunched over in the cold night air.

"Hi."

"Let's go in. I'm freezing."

They stepped inside, the contrast of the warmth wonderfully overwhelming. Millie saw an empty table littered with dirty glasses and plates and went straight towards it. They put their coats around the backs of the chairs and sat down.

The band members were placing their instruments in stands in the corner to take a break as jukebox music took up the slack. A waitress came over and took their order.

"So, Naomi, I really wanted to thank you. Really, it was so kind of you. I was really out of it."

"You seemed out of it. You kept asking me my name over and over. I'm just glad you're okay."

They talked over the details of the accident in the way that people talk about something when they fear they have nothing else to talk about. Luckily for Naomi, Millie was one of those women who really knew how to talk, and Naomi found herself both listening and prompting. Millie didn't need too much prompting.

When the story of the accident, including the details of the very cute Officer Millerton, the awkwardness of wearing a neck brace, being on a back board en route to the hospital, the very abrasive woman from the pickup truck, and insurance company issues were elaborated upon far beyond their conversational value, there was a moment of silence during which they both sipped their red wine.

"Well, so what do you do, Naomi? Do you work?"

"Yes, I work at Ida's Bakery." Naomi immediately felt herself tense up, an old crusty feeling that came when anyone asked anything which might reveal who she was. Old insecurities prevailed tonight.

"Ida's? I love Ida's. She makes the best stuff."

"She does. I get to eat that stuff on a daily basis, and it's beginning to show."

Millie laughed. "Well, I teach second grade at the elementary school. I grew up here and then went to school in St. Paul. But I always knew I'd come back here. I got married after I graduated with my teaching degree."

"You're married?"

"No, he was a creep. It only lasted four years. I met him when we were in school. When the reality of life set in, I realized it was a mistake. So we got divorced, and I moved back here. I kept his name though. Bing was his name."

"Why'd you keep it?"

"Bing. Such a great name. Bing Crosby. Bing cherries. Anything is better than being a Johnson in this state."

Naomi laughed. "Well, my last name gets a lot of questions. Blue."

"What kind of last name is that? Blue?"

"My immigrant great-grandfather came in through Ellis Island. His name was Isadore Blaustein. An immigration official accidentally changed it to Bluestein. And later, Izzie changed it to

Blue, to sound more American. I was teased a lot in junior high school about my name. It might have just been better to have stuck to the original."

"No, I like it. It's better than Blaustein. Have you ever been married?"

"Nope." Naomi hoped a simple response would work, but Millie was more inquisitive than most of the Minnesotans she'd met, and she dreaded the fact that there might be more questions.

"No? Well, any serious relationships?"

"Sure. I've had some. I lived with a guy once. It didn't last. We were too different, I guess."

Millie stopped fishing for information. Naomi hoped her terse answers would slow Millie down. Naomi drank some wine. She had been with Will for eight years, living in Maryland. When they met, he was a graduate student at the university in the school of criminal justice while she worked in various jobs, supporting them both on her slightly more than minimum wages. Loving Will came easily. She had not been with a man who was so good to her, who shared all the household chores with her, except cleaning toilets. He listened to Naomi at the end of the day. He passed her tissues when she cried for no reason. He rubbed lotion onto her back and massaged her muscles until she slept. And then one day she came home early from work with a fever and saw the yellow Volkswagen Beetle parked in her spot, a pair of leather sandals inside the front door, and ten perfectly polished rose-colored fingernails at the end of slender arms, wrapped around Will's back, in Naomi and Will's bed, in the middle of the afternoon. That was the moment that all Will's goodness was eclipsed by his utter deceit. Naomi had stood in the doorway of their bedroom, white-faced and stunned into stone. The woman had looked around Will's shoulder at her with eyes that Naomi will never forget—defiant and possessive. Before Will stopped his thrusting Naomi was gone, taking only her hiking boots from the front hall closet. She would not negotiate any terms of continuing her relationship to Will. His attempts to be forgiven, his explanation of what had really happened, how little the woman meant to him, his proclamation of his deep love for her, his offer of counseling, and his promise to be faithful were written in notes attached to flowers (five bouquets and two arrangements in vases), in emails sent daily, and in cell phone messages too long to listen all the way through. Naomi felt the woman's eyes on her as brutal testimony of what Naomi did not have: sex in the middle of the afternoon. It had been one of Will's quirks that he only made love to her in complete darkness. She could not ever forgive this.

"So what happened?" Millie asked.

"It's a long story. No, really, it isn't. He cheated on me in the middle of the afternoon and I found them together."

"Ugh. That's the worst. You think you'll ever get married?"

"Who knows. It's not on my list of important things to do."

"So what is?"

Naomi laughed. "Getting some furniture in my house, for starters. I left that afternoon with nothing. Really. I could use some furniture." Laughing, Millie lifted her glass up. Naomi met it.

HENRY ALEXANDER

HENRY WATCHED THE TABLE of women during the band's break, deciding which one he might like, drawn to the one whose shirt was open revealing more than a little cleavage, and yet also drawn to the one who seemed to engage the other women with her stories. And of course, he also liked the one who was laughing and completely at ease with herself. And then he saw Millie Bing and the woman from the bakery sitting together at a table.

Henry knew this feeling, this feeling of being gripped by a stranger. It wasn't something he could articulate, just something he knew happened once in a long while. It was a feeling of being both intrigued and hooked, clearly a part of it involuntary. He watched the women, wondering how they knew each other. Millie seemed to be doing most of the talking, and the other woman—what was her name—awkwardly sitting, listening. Henry sat there watching the women. Being slightly tipsy, he did not trust himself to go over to them. It was midnight before he watched them pay their bill, leave a few dollars on the table, and walk out the door, without ever seeing him. Whether it was the beer or the woman making him not think clearly, he didn't know.

Chapter Seven

Ida Minsky

Ida was alone in the bakery, her dough long since risen, and was beginning to make cinnamon bread. She brushed a mixture of melted butter and milk across the flattened sheets of dough. Then she sprinkled the cinnamon—from Ceylon, its taste sweet and tangy—across the dough. She had rolled up four of the loaves when there was a knocking at the front door. She glanced up at the clock above the counter. It was barely 5:15 a.m. Who would be at the door? The lights weren't on in the front yet, but the dim reflection from the streetlight showed the figure of a man peering in the big front window. A chill crept up Ida's back, damp from working hard on her bread.

"Ida!" she heard. "Open up."

She recognized the voice. Rooster Robinson. She rushed to the door and flipped the deadbolt and opened the door.

"What is it? What's wrong?" she exclaimed.

"Wrong? Why do you think something is wrong?" he answered, coming through the door without being asked.

Ida was speechless for a moment. She was confused by his early appearance at her door, yet also delighted. But why was he here?

"You come bursting in, you do, knocking on my door before the sun rises, and you ask me why I think something is wrong?"

"Yes, my apology, Mrs. Minsky, Ida, my apologies. I, uh, yes, my apologies. Forgiveness, yes, forgiveness, I ask—"

"Enough, Mr. Robinson. Enough. What is it?"

He hesitated. "It is . . . it is just that . . ."

She waited.

"Just that I wanted to see you. Just see you. I have not been sleeping well, Mrs. Minsky. Not since the day you graced me with your presence looking for pecans and ground beef."

"Hmph. Are you mocking me?"

"No, Mrs. Minsky. I would not mock you. I don't understand it myself. I just wanted to see you. I came here, the next day, did you know? I came here to taste your cake, to taste the pecans turned into something marvelous. The girl was here. You were not. But I wanted to see you."

Ida was completely surprised, perhaps even embarrassed. She was not sure what to say or what to do. When all else fails, she knew, serve cake.

"Mr. Robinson, would you like a piece of cake now? It's day old, but ach, still good. I can make some coffee?"

"Yes, Mrs. Minsky. That would be very good."

"Sit down. You're making me nervous."

NAOMI BLUE

NAOMI BLUE NEEDED TO FACE the fact that the paycheck she got from working at the bakery was not much. The house was still sparsely decorated. To be honest, it wasn't really decorated at all. She spent most of her time in just two rooms of the house—the bedroom and the kitchen. But she owned her own home and felt quite a bit of pride in that. It didn't matter all that much to her that there was no place to sit in the living room and that the dining room was empty except for the glass chandelier, an object that collected far more dust than she thought possible in an empty house. This house was a good place to start fresh. But a little more money wouldn't hurt.

There would be a time for decorating, Naomi Blue presumed. But with a long stretch of Minnesota winter approaching, she decided to see about getting a warm coat at the Carriage General. The Carriage General was just down the street from Ida's Bakery. She put Beatrix on a leash and headed down there. It was common practice in Copper Prairie to tie dogs—and an occasional ferret—to the parking meter posts in front of the stores. The meters were no longer used to regulate parking. As an experiment at raising funds, the meters had been unsuccessful at doing much more than irritating the snowplowing farmers who showed their refusal to pay the meters by pulling their pickups in a bit too far. Most of the meters now stood at a forty-five degree angle. The cost of meter removal and sidewalk repair had come up exactly eight times in as many years at the city eldermen's meetings. Voting the thousands necessary for this project so far remained an "extraordinary expense" and a cost suitable for "the Cities" not for a small community like Copper Prairie. Other town projects consumed the council, including the war memorial statue in the park in the center of town and the beautiful arched welcome on the south side, hoping to welcome travelers coming up from the Cities who might not have thought of stopping for a good meal in Copper Prairie. The Lions Welcome You. Rotary Meets Here. Tree City USA.

Naomi Blue tied Beatrix up at the meter in front of the Carriage General and told her to stay. Of course Beatrix would stay, but the command gave her a job to do, kept her dog mind occupied. Naomi pushed open the door.

"Hello there, miss. How are you today?" The man greeted her in that genuinely friendly way of small towns, where storeowners wait on customers themselves and know the importance of customer service. He seemed to be an ancient man. The lines in his face created concentric rings of expression around his eyes and cheeks. His neck was vaguely reminiscent of the skin on the back end of a fryer chicken from Robinson's. His eyes were frosted green, the haze of age clouding what must have been startling green eyes at one time.

"I'm fine," Naomi replied.

"Can I help you find something?"

"No thanks, I'm going to look around."

Naomi didn't want to give away what she was there for. It would be much more fun to try on shoes, hats, and sweaters than just coats. She could pretend to have money.

Naomi walked slowly down the planked wood floors of the store. Men's clothes were on the left, women's on the right. Glass topped display cases in the back of the store showcased an odd assortment of silver jewelry, some with turquoise stones, some in twisted silver, a few pieces tarnished with age. There were boxes of shoes in the back corner, a mixture of work boots, running shoes and sandals. A cardboard box full of assorted shoes with the words handwritten "$10 A PAIR" caught Naomi's attention. Shoes were tumbled in the box, but if you could find one shoe in your size, chances were good its mate was in there too. She picked out a teal-colored cowboy boot, a pink bedroom slipper, and a black biker's boot with a heavy zipper up the side. It could be fun to have those cowboy boots, and they were her size, but they were simply too teal.

Naomi looked through the circular racks of sweaters and fleece and noticed an off-white wool fisherman's sweater. Only in a size small.

"I was wondering if you have this in a medium?" Naomi said to the storekeeper.

"Well, I believe I do. I think it's on the manikin up front."

Together they walked to the front of the store. The manikin was up in the window and Naomi realized the effort it would take for the man to get there.

"Would you like me to go up there and get the sweater?"

"Yes, my dear, that would be nice. I have people to do my window display. I'm a bit shaky to climb up there. And if I made it up there, I might not make it back down."

Naomi Blue began to undress the manikin. It was a peculiar feeling to be standing in the window, with people walking by. She had a sudden urge to stand still and pose. She put her hands in the same awkward position of the manikin, raised one hip by angling her foot toe down, and looked out the window, fixing her eyes blankly on the bank building's awning. She stayed still for a few moments, until the storekeeper interrupted her posing.

"Would you mind putting this other sweater on the manikin instead, miss? I don't want her catching cold in the window."

Naomi Blue felt completely exposed. What was she thinking?

The manikin properly dressed, Naomi tried on the fisherman sweater in front of the mirror. She loved it. The cable knitting down the front, the softness of the wool, this was better than a winter jacket. But just as expensive.

"Looks very nice on you," the man said.

Naomi Blue smiled and fished out some money from her pocket. As the man rang up the sale, he looked Naomi over a bit more closely than Naomi thought necessary.

"I liked that, I did. I liked the posing you did in the window."

Naomi said nothing. Her embarrassment overpowered her irritation at what might be a rather strange attempt at a pass.

"Sales have been rather slow this fall, and I wonder, well, odd as this sounds, I wonder if you might want a part-time job modeling. In the window, that is. I could put you in some of the clothes here and you could, you know, model them. I've seen that done before, live models . . . I know this sounds a little strange, out of the blue, but maybe it would be good for business."

Naomi glanced back over at the window.

"Could I be paid in clothes?"

The man held out his hand. "It's a deal. My name is Sebastian Skinner."

Naomi took his dry hand in hers. "I'm Naomi Blue. Deal."

Naomi left Carriage General wearing her new fisherman sweater with a plan to return later in the week for her first modeling job.

Sebastian Skinner

Sebastian Skinner looked down at his hand as the girl left the store. What was her name again? The touch of her hand in his had sparked some vague threads of memory. He drifted back to an image of Wanda Cooper, Wanda, young and flirty, avoiding his eyes as she placed ten dollars in his hand, payment for a wool jersey dress, ten dollars that most people would have placed on the counter, but not Wanda. She would rather have touched his hand, have pretended not to notice that she had touched him, such innocent physical contact. What was this girl's name? His memory was clear for Wanda and for anything that happened years ago. It was just the immediate bits of information that he lost, as if they never made it into his mind. He was aware of this oddness, of the way he lost perspective of time, of how Wanda was becoming clearer in his mind and some of the details of people he saw on a daily basis were becoming fuzzy. It was something he accepted without concern. In fact, he much preferred the warmth he felt when the past drifted forward into the present.

Henry Alexander

Henry had come to a conclusion. Running for office was not something he wanted to do. Actually being in office was another story—he did want to do that. But campaigning, from what he was able to figure out, involved door knocking. Door knocking meant walking, greeting people, and talking to people. At the top of his list of concerns about talking to people was what to talk about since he didn't quite know what he believed in. He believed in a lot of lofty ideals, but he wasn't sure which of these were relevant to Copper Prairie. And he didn't know how to give the impression that he was a serious candidate to this community of people he didn't really know. Why would they believe that he had their best interests in mind when he had no idea what their best interests were? He only knew that he wanted the town of Copper Prairie to be environmentally friendly. His idealism had given him the confidence to run for office and the belief that he could be a good city elder, despite his twenty-nine years, more than half of them spent in school. His confidence flagging, Henry decided that he would run by not running. He wouldn't actually campaign.

He also decided to get a cup of coffee at Ida's. His preoccupation with running for city elder had only moderately subdued his growing interest in the woman who worked at the bakery. He was beginning to see her around town every few days, and this was fueling his attraction. Sometimes he saw her walking a big dog. Once he even followed her in his car and only turned around when he realized that she was headed to the John Moore Road, which was too isolated for her not to notice him trailing her. He wondered if she were walking through the cemetery. He also saw her walking past Mikey's in the late afternoon, clearly her path home from Ida's Bakery. He was beginning to know her routines. It wasn't that Henry was trying to know her routines—it was just unavoidable. The woman walked everywhere in the small town, and his lack of any real occupation left him with time to notice. And she kept showing up with her long hair, tight shirts, and those curves. Yes, the woman preoccupied him, and he was growing obsessed with wanting to know her. He could shut his eyes and visualize the way she walked, how she looked down at the ground in front of her, how she didn't seem to wear warm enough clothes, her breasts so commanding. When he was wearing his wool cap and a coat, she was still wearing just a sweater. He knew she talked to her dog as they walked. He knew she didn't have a car. He knew she lived on the west side of Copper Prairie, though he hadn't yet had the nerve to figure out where exactly. And with all that he knew, Henry was aware that he knew nothing about her. Not her name, not her age, not her story. He didn't even know enough to explain this attraction. But sometimes women did this to him. They caught him. He knew the appeal was physical . . . her hair, her breasts, and the mystery. Henry felt bound to her in some peculiar way. But he knew that as he got to know women, the attraction faded and he would be left with two visions of the woman—the reality of the person who didn't interest him, and the imaginary vision of this sexy fascinating woman who stood off in the distance. He fell for the magic of the unknown. Ignoring all reason and self-doubt, Henry went to see her again at the bakery.

IDA MINSKY

IDA MINSKY'S RESTLESS NIGHTS had worsened. The repeated dreams of childhood had begun to fade. And while she was relieved by this, having believed that such dreams came to old women before they died, the dreams were not replaced with restful sleep. They were replaced by dreams the likes of which she hadn't had for many years. She dreamed of a man touching her, loving her, bringing her close to release, but not quite. She awoke in the night, restless and aroused. She could not visualize the man's features, nor see him in her mind. But she was aware of a vaguely familiar wakefulness in her body and mind that had not been present for a long time. She did not think deeply about these dreams, knowing that Rooster Robinson was the obvious cause of them. His continued interest piqued her. In so many ways, he was not a man that she would be interested in. First, he was old and looked it. Despite Ida's own years, she did not often look into the mirror and so had no concept that she too looked that "old." The apartment's small bathroom had the only mirror and it had long ago been infiltrated by the mistiness of time. When she caught a glance of herself in the reflection in the big oven door, she noticed only her girth. She didn't notice the lines of time and age that had softened her face. Rooster, however, looked old. And he was short. Sure, Ida was short as well, but that wasn't relevant. What was relevant was the fact that he cleared her by a mere three inches. But Rooster Robinson was a big man by behavior. He sucked air into his barrel chest and swaggered through her dreams. Ida knew she could not talk herself out of the wild thoughts that were beginning to sneak into her waking hours as well.

Naomi Blue

Naomi looked up from behind the coffee urn where she had just poured herself a cup of fresh coffee during a slow moment in the bakery. It was that guy again, Henry Morgan Alexander, the one running for city elder.

"Hi," Henry said to Naomi. "How are things here at the bakery?"

"Oh, they're doing okay. What can I get you?" All business.

"I'd love a cup of coffee, for sure. Let me see . . . I would like something to go with it too."

Naomi fixed his coffee while Henry decided. She felt his eyes on her. He wasn't looking at the pastries at all, she knew.

"What have you decided on?"

"How about that, the scone," he said pointing. "What's in it?"

"It's apricot and cranberry. It's really good."

"And what isn't?" he laughed, taking the scone and coffee over to a table.

"It's all good, you're right," Naomi said.

Henry sat down at a table. He broke a piece off the scone.

"So, what's your name, anyway? I think if I'm going to be a regular, I should know your name."

"Naomi Blue."

"That's your whole name? Naomi Blue? Blue as in the color?"

This was just the kind of reaction that for years had made Naomi crazy. She used to have all sorts of smart responses for it, mostly at the maturity level of a ten-year old. No, she'd say sarcastically, blue as in the color of your eye when I punch you out. There had been ruder responses for the boys.

"Yes. Naomi Blue." She no longer said the things she thought.

"Wow, that's a great name. I'm Henry."

"Henry Morgan Alexander, right?"

"Hey, how did you know that?"

"Well, you're the guy running for city elder, aren't you? They ran a profile of all the candidates in the *Copper Press*."

"Ah, yes. That would be me."

"What made you decide to run for city elder, anyway? Do you think you have a chance? Some of your opposition have a few years on you."

"I don't know. I want to make a difference, change things, and just make things happen around here. So I filed the papers. Now I'm not so sure it was such a great idea."

"Well, why not. You've got my vote. I haven't met any of the other candidates. Maybe they buy their coffee and breakfast at the QuikStop."

"Thanks for your confidence."

Naomi was rarely this friendly to customers. Actually, she was rarely this friendly to anyone in Copper Prairie. But Henry seemed harmless. And she knew that Ida would be listening with pleasure at the banter.

Chapter Eight

Naomi Blue

Naomi's next day off from the bakery was her first day of modeling at the Carriage General. The morning started off rough. The early freight train was a long one. One of the vases on the dresser crashed to the floor and then rolled towards the dog's bed, startling Beatrix who jumped in fright onto Naomi's bed. The dog's seventy-five pounds caused Naomi to slide in towards the middle of the bed towards the dog, who then placed her head on the extra pillow beside Naomi. Naomi Blue rolled on her side away from the dog. There was something downright weird about a dog lying beside her in bed.

To make the morning even more difficult, Sebastian Skinner at the Carriage General did not seem to remember who Naomi Blue was or anything related to their conversation about her modeling.

"Mr. Skinner, hi. I'm here to model."

"You're here to what?"

"Um, model. Remember? I'm Naomi Blue. Model? In the window?"

Sebastian Skinner rubbed his forehead, as if to shake loose the memories of the prior week.

"Sweetheart, remind me."

Naomi was tempted, ever so tempted, to say she was teasing, to forget the whole arrangement. The days that had passed had left her regretting this agreement. She was not the kind of girl who modeled; she wasn't thin or pretty or confident enough to stand in the window of a store and model. Models came from a different sort of mold. But her desire for some income, even if it were in the form of new clothes, was enough to overcome her insecurities.

"I bought the fisherman knit sweater, remember? And I took it off the manikin in the window, and then you thought it might be a good idea if—"

"Ah, yes, yes, now I remember. Yes. Right. You're my model."

"Yes, I guess so, that's me."

Sebastian Skinner walked off towards the back of the store. Naomi Blue followed silently. It was too late for the misgivings that were rapidly becoming a problem in the way of a flush of nerves up her neck. Sebastian Skinner pulled clothes off of a few racks, went behind the glass counter to find a few more things and finally held out a pile of clothing to Naomi.

"Here. Wear this. I think it will be the cat's meow."

Naomi Blue nodded and went into the curtained dressing room to change. It was too late to change her mind. A skirt, a blouse, a sweater, a pair of shoes and a necklace. She emerged, hoping to find a mirror before Sebastian Skinner would see her. She stood, turned and sighed. She wasn't exactly transformed, but it was a different Naomi staring back at her in the mirror.

"Yes, indeed, very nice. Very nice. You look like a woman now. Curvy. Not like that manikin."

Naomi knew he meant it as a compliment, but she had never learned to like her curves. She walked carefully in the high heels to the front of the store. Here goes, she thought, as she stepped up into the window. She walked to the other side of the window, opposite the manikin who maintained her place in the display. Maybe it was being in the window again, or maybe it was the outfit, perhaps the heels, but she was overwhelmed by that same odd feeling she'd had the first time she posed in the window. She tipped her hip, turning out her right foot, adjusted her skirt, glanced quickly down, found a comfortable position for her hands, and looked across to the bank.

The street was quiet. Naomi adjusted herself to find a few different positions that would allow her to be still but keep her muscles loose. And then she fell into this strange state, a kind of separation between her body and her mind. It was as if she were watching herself from the street, glancing up at the flesh-and-blood person behind the window. Her mind hovered beyond the window. But just as Naomi Blue was experiencing her first out of body experience of sorts, watching herself, someone actually was watching her. She didn't notice the person there at first, so distant was she from her body, staring off at the bank in her mind's eye. But suddenly, she saw him. Like looking away from a star to see it more clearly, she could see him standing a few yards from the window, staring at her. At first, he stood as still as she stood. Neither of them blinked. Then he neared the window.

Naomi Blue felt his eyes. She ignored them. Model, she thought, just model. Be still. An itch threatened her composure. Ignore it, she told herself. Perhaps she knew him.

Soon, there was a small gathering of people in front of the Carriage General. She shifted into another position, in a slow shift of limbs. There were smiles. She remained still again. People moved on. Naomi remained.

Finally, Naomi Blue came out of the window. She sat down immediately and removed the heels. Sebastian Skinner was smiling.

"Very good, Miss Blue. Very good. You were so still, so quiet, like a statue, you were. Very good."

"It was weird up there. But okay."

When Naomi Blue walked out of the store that day, she had under her arms the teal cowboy boots. It seemed only appropriate that she choose the wildest thing in the store that day.

Henry Alexander

As luck would have it, Henry was passing by the Carriage General at precisely the hour that Naomi Blue was modeling. Since his dreams were already filled with her, since he saw her everywhere he went whether it was her or not, he wasn't immediately sure that it truly was the woman up there in the window. This could just be another one of his fantasies. But even from across the street he recognized her ample shape. He stopped in mid step. He crossed the street to get a better look. He came closer. It was Naomi Blue, the woman from the bakery. He could not believe his eyes. She was so still, so utterly calm, and so poised, it was hard to believe this was the same person. And he couldn't believe that he could stare at her without compunction. And stare he did. She kept her eyes high, looking into the distance. Henry was fixed in his spot on the sidewalk until he was no longer alone. People around him were exclaiming, "Isn't that great?" "She's fabulous, so still." "Mom, is she real?" "Yes dear, she is. She's modeling."

She had a quality about her that Henry couldn't explain. It wasn't beauty. No, it wasn't that at all, but it was something. It was something of a sexy look, attractive and different. *I'm bewitched*, he thought, *and I need to know her, I need to touch her.* Henry had not thought of himself as particularly foolish up until this point; he felt grounded, logical, analytical, and absolutely reasonable. But with this woman, things were going another direction. As he walked away from Naomi Blue standing in the window display, he knew he was smitten. How ridiculous, he thought. *Keep cool, Henry, keep cool. You're running for city elder. Eldermen don't go crazy after women who model in store windows. Come on, man, settle down.*

IDA MINSKY

At that same moment, Ida Minsky was also telling herself what to think and who she was. It was working just as poorly. She had been quite happy in her small bakery world, working hard, hands immersed in flour and butter and sugar each dawn, watching the street from her chair in the window, crawling into bed to her dreams early each night. But now she was being courted, and courted quite actively. Rooster Robinson, this grouchy short old man was being sweet and polite, and coming by the bakery twice a day for coffee and treats. She was sure he'd turn into a fat short old man if this kept up too long.

She was formal towards him, a bit curt even, but she loved his attention. It had been a long time since she'd felt feminine, since she'd tied her hair up differently, a loose chignon maybe, since she paid much attention to how she looked in the morning. But a man's attention can have this impact on a woman, and Ida knew she had fallen into that space. It had just been so long.

She was unsure, however, of the time such a courtship should take these days. As a girl, much time elapsed before she would have let a man hold her hand, kiss her cheek—to say nothing about the lips—and go further. Much time. *These days, ach,* she thought, *I don't know how this should go. He's old,* she thought. *But I am old too.* What would he think of her? How would it be? And then what about Copper Prairie? What would people think? Ida Minsky and Rooster Robinson? Did she even care what people thought? Ida sighed out loud. *I'm too old to care what they think. Let them talk.*

Chapter Nine

Naomi Blue

Wednesdays at the bakery were usually a little quieter than the rest of the week. And Wednesdays on a cold blustery October day were even quieter. No customers came in by nine o'clock and Ida came out from the back.

"It's very quiet in here."

"Yes, it is. It feels like winter, doesn't it, Ida?"

"Too soon for winter. But snow isn't a stranger to October up here. Remember the winter of '76?"

"Uh, I wasn't here for that winter."

"Ach, it was a snow like I had never seen in all my years. It started at three o'clock and didn't stop until the next evening. I didn't leave the building for days. But when the fellas shoveled the sidewalks, business was very good. Yes, I was busy, baking and glazing, chopping, what a time that was. Nearly three feet of snow in October, yes, it can happen, it can happen."

Just as Ida returned to the ovens in the back to check on the baguettes, the door opened. In walked Henry, with a bright-green campaign button on his jacket with white print that read: Henry Morgan Alexander 4 City Elder.

"Hello, Naomi Blue."

"Hi," she responded, looking at the button. "Are you out campaigning today?"

"Yes, well, I thought I'd win over the business community, so I'm going door to door talking to the store owners. It's been very interesting."

"How so?" Naomi asked.

"Well, first, they all laugh. They think I'm kidding and tell me I'm too young and probably not as conservative as the bunch in office."

Naomi laughed. "I bet that's true."

"And then, when I tell them why I'm running, most of them talk about what bugs them, what they want to see changed, about their taxes, about parking problems, garbage collection and so on . . . it's been very enlightening."

"Do you want to talk to Mrs. Minsky?"

"Well, yes, but no. I mean, I, yes. But first, well," Henry was tongue-tied beyond belief. Naomi wondered how he could ever be city elder if he couldn't articulate a simple sentence. "Actually, Naomi, I want to talk to you first."

"Okay, you are."

"I mean, uh, well, what I'm trying to say is, would you go out with me? Take a walk sometime? Just hang out or something?"

"Sure," Naomi replied, more in an effort to get him to relax than a real desire to have a date with this guy. He was just a kid. Cute, but still, she'd already determined that he was too young to actually date. "How about we go for a walk? I have this big dog at home that needs exercise and maybe we can walk her together."

"That would be great!" Henry said, his voice unusually loud. "When works for you?"

"How about later, when I'm out of here. Four?"

"It's a plan, Naomi."

As Henry left, Naomi started to stop him, since he had forgotten to speak to Ida Minsky. Then she realized he probably never meant to speak to her at all.

Henry Alexander

Henry was relieved. He had finally managed to ask Naomi out and she had said yes, more or less. It wasn't an actual date, but he was going to see her. He needed to be with her. This need was turning into an obsession and he hoped that spending some time with her would quell this seemingly uncontrollable force. He hoped.

He was mortified, however, by how inarticulate he became around her. She seemed to turn off the part of his brain needed for communication. It was both predictable and embarrassing. He prayed that he'd regain his composure by the afternoon. Of course he would. She was just a woman, just the bakery girl, she was just . . . Forget it, he thought. Just relax and meet her as planned.

Ida Minsky

Ah, thought Ida, listening in the back. *The young man likes my Naomi Blue, does he?* He certainly seemed nervous enough talking to her. Running for city elder? Just a child. Well, let him run, this city could do with some fresh blood, some fresh thinking. Maybe he would shake things up a bit in this sleepy town. Not that she minded it sleepy, hah, but it could be quite set in its ways, run by a bunch of old men. Ida might be old, and maybe even wise, but that kid seems smart enough with his youthful ideals. Let the boy win. Hmph.

When the bakery was closed for the day, Ida felt a terrible weariness in her legs. She slowly climbed the stairs to her apartment, kicked off her shoes at the door, started over to her chair, and then turned back to neatly line her shoes up in the closet. She padded over to the chair facing the window, unbuttoned her skirt, and collapsed into the chair. After putting her feet up on the ottoman, Ida let out a low groan and fell into the deep sleep of exhaustion.

It was dark outside when she woke with a start, confused whether it was night or just before dawn. And then she heard the banging at the door downstairs. A rapid sequence of thumps and a deep voice saying, "Ida, you there? Ida? Ida!"

She got up, her hips stiff. She walked to the door, buttoned up her skirt, listening.

"Ida? It's Roger. You there?"

Roger? Rooster. What was he all in a dither about, she wondered. She flipped on the stairwell light and went down. Rooster Robinson's face was bright red, the cold air whipping the leaves in circles behind him.

"Ida," he gasped. "You're okay."

"Why wouldn't I be? What are you doing here? What is wrong with you?"

"I just thought—well—I wanted to be sure, it was dark in there, the windows were dark, the bakery dark, and I . . ."

It's quite possible that Rooster would have come in had Ida invited him, or if she had moved just a bit to one side of the doorframe. As it was, she hardly left any room for him to consider coming in uninvited.

Still shaking off sleep, Ida was trying to remember if she had planned to meet Roger this evening or not. Not, she decided.

"I'm tired, Roger. I must have fallen asleep. What time is it?"

"Mrs. Minsky, Ida, I beg your pardon. I wanted to see you and I looked up at your window, your window, I know you close your shades and they were open and it was dark and I thought, how silly of me, please, excuse my boldness, but I thought, something was wrong, the curtains, you see." And with this admission of his spying, as Ida clearly saw it, of knowing her patterns, he took her hand in his, pleading for her forgiveness.

"You are so cold, Roger, come in." The man was both exasperating and endearing. Before she had a chance to open the door to the bakery, he was climbing the stairs to her apartment. No man had ever been there, no man except the plumber and that half-drunk electrician. No man on a social call. He was halfway up before she realized that she had little choice but to follow him up and hope the wrinkles were smoothed out of the bedspread.

Rooster Robinson waited as Ida turned on more lamps, and set about to put up the kettle for tea. Rooster was suddenly awkward in his realization that this apartment was little more than an efficiency and that he had found himself in Ida Minsky's living room, kitchen and without question, her bedroom, all at the same time.

Ida was awkward for all the same reasons, but with her back to him as she fixed them a snack, she could hide her embarrassment. Tea, she thought to herself, fix the tea, slice up some apple cake, make him comfortable, be normal, and act gracious. He is a good man, a little stubborn, a little crazy maybe, but a good man.

They sat across from each other, the tea still too hot to drink.

"How come you know that I shut my shades? How come you're looking up here?" Ida couldn't resist teasing him.

Rooster Robinson blushed, something Ida would have bet he didn't do often. He slurped his tea, trying to avoid a quick answer.

"I, ah, it's been, I ah, hmph." The room was quiet again. Rooster tried once more. "Ever since that day in the store, ever since the day you knocked over my soup cans, I wanted to talk more with you. I don't know why, but, well, you were just there, there in my mind."

"I see," Ida said. She did see. That was the day she stopped being the limping old woman who owned the bakery and became just woman. Ida wasn't sure exactly how she felt about this, though her stomach had become a little jumpy. Rooster wasn't such a bad looking guy for someone his age, Ida thought, reminding herself that she was about his age. Maybe he was having similar thoughts about her as well. She looked at him more closely. He could use a little grooming, she noticed, with those white shoots of bristly hair coming out from his ears and a wildness about his right eyebrow. But Ida was not one to judge too harshly, and it had been a long time since a man had sat across from her having tea. *We will just have to see where this goes*, she thought wryly, *we will just have to see.*

As Ida drank her tea, picking at her piece of cake, she partly looked out the window as she would normally do alone, and partly watched Rooster. *He is eating my cake like a hungry man, a sloppy eater. Ach, no one feeds the man.* With his plate empty, Rooster leaned back in his chair.

"Ida, your stuff, your food, I mean, your cake is fantastic. The best." He stumbled over his words. Ida smiled.

"Thank you, Rooster."

"Maybe you can call me Roger? Would that be okay?"

"Of course. Where did the name Rooster come from, anyway?"

A gruff sound emitted from his throat as he ran his hand through his still thick hair.

"It was partly this hair, which used to be more red than white. And partly my way with the girls. I liked them all."

"Oh?" Ida wasn't sure what to say to this.

"I liked them all but got none. I was left alone to crow."

Ida laughed. "I shall call you Roger then."

"Good, I'd like that."

Soon after, Ida stood up, smoothing her skirt. Roger stood as well.

"Thank you, Ida, for tea and for, well, humoring me."

"You're welcome. But you don't need to worry if my shades are open."

Roger looked down at his shoes, embarrassed again. They walked down the hallway stairs slowly. Just as Ida was about to close the door, Roger leaned back in and gave her a dry peck on the cheek.

"Thank you, Ida," he said and disappeared into the dark.

Ida hadn't been kissed in more years than she could count. She touched her cheek where his lips had been and wondered what had just happened.

Naomi Blue

Naomi's acquiescence to go on a walk with Henry had happened for two specific reasons. The first was the decision she had made to be social. She felt she ought to be a part of Copper Prairie and not be such a loner. Why not walk? The other reason for the walk was the fact that Naomi was amused by Henry's attentiveness. He seemed so eager to do something with her, so interested, looking at her with those eyes, maybe a little pathetic. She told herself she could quell his interest by going out with him, maybe even get rid of him. She did not admit her interest in him.

As she walked home from the bakery, she began to wonder whether she had time to shower before meeting him, what she would wear, and then of course, chastising herself for caring about how she looked on a silly walk. But his interest in her was flattering, even if he was ten years younger, even if she never let it go any further. It was definitely flattering.

Naomi did shower, telling herself it was to get rid of the smell of the bakery and not because she wanted to clean up for Henry. In a definitive effort not to look like she cared about impressing him, she put on the big blue Buffalo sweatshirt over a pair of patched jeans. She hardly even fooled herself.

Just as she came downstairs, she heard the knock at the door. She realized it was the first time since she'd lived there that anyone had come to the door.

"Hi, my name is Henry Alexander and I'm running for city elder." Henry stuck out his hand.

Naomi laughed. She shook it firmly.

"Why the hell are you running for city elder?"

"Good question."

Naomi put the leash on Beatrix, who was busy sniffing Henry and wagging her tail in delight at someone new to play with. They headed out down the sidewalk towards John Moore Road, away from town. For a short while, they were quiet. They began to relax and talk. Naomi told Henry about Beatrix and her sudden appearance. Henry talked about his campaign. He talked about growing up in Copper Prairie. He talked about Minneapolis clubs, St. Paul coffee shops, about his parents moving to Arizona, about coming home to Copper Prairie. And before they even reached the cemetery, it was clear there was going to be no shortage of conversation between them.

What also became clear to Naomi Blue was Henry's desire for her. His hand brushed hers too often to be accidental. He began to walk closer, bumping her ever so slightly. His words became less conversational and more nuanced and suggestive. She could feel the physical tension building between them. Naomi told herself that the electricity between them was something he was creating, a charge he was causing, an energy he was emitting, not her, no way, not her. And yet. Naomi wasn't ready to admit that she found him interesting as well as sexy. *He's too young for me*, she kept telling herself as they walked. *I could never be involved with someone in his twenties. I could never take my clothes off in front of someone so much younger, I couldn't. It's crazy.*

They circled through the cemetery, looking at the oldest stones, commenting on the Scandinavian and German names on the majority of the markers. Naomi let Beatrix off the leash and she went from tombstone to tombstone, sniffing the sides of the stones excitedly.

"I'm so glad we went for this walk, Naomi."

"Yeah, this is fun." Naomi kept the conversation light. She pretended to be interested in a stone engraving from 1936. He came closer. She shoved her hands in her front sweatshirt pocket. He wanted something, she knew. He was trying to get closer. She moved back.

"You seem nervous," Henry said. "Jumpy."

"Oh, you know, cemeteries."

"Uh huh," Henry paused. "What would you do if I kissed you?"

"Kissed me?" Naomi had to stall. What would she do? Her lack of response created a long pause for Henry—so long a pause that he clearly decided it meant a kiss was okay. Before she could even get her hands out of her pocket, he took her face in his hands, so gently, and bent down to kiss her. His warmth so close to her was powerful. She kissed him back.

He drew away to look at her.

"You didn't wait for my answer," she said.

"I didn't think I had to."

They walked back to town quietly. Naomi's mind was racing and she couldn't think of anything to say. *He's too young. Nice kiss. He's way too young. Nice guy. He's so much younger. Interesting, sexy. Can I do this? So young . . . who cares.*

Chapter Ten

Henry Alexander

When they arrived back at Naomi's house, she clearly wasn't interested in his coming in. He had been hoping for an invitation, a cup of tea, something, anything—but she had not said much on the way back. She had easily opened up when they set out on their walk. Naomi told him about her mother, Dora, who lived in Costa Rica. She talked about her past relationships. She talked about her father's death. She told him about working for Ida Minsky. They had definitely connected, he knew. But the kiss had shifted things. Damn! Why did he have to do that? It had been going so well.

Maybe he had been too forward in kissing her, although he was sure she enjoyed it. The silence concerned him. But she had kissed him right back. Really kissed him. Then she had become so quiet, and the balance between them seemed upset. He didn't regret the kiss. His mind played the moment over and over. The kiss told him everything he wanted to know. She felt it. He knew it. And now he had to have more.

He had to kiss her again. She was making him crazy. He needed to kiss her again. He needed the contact. As he made his way back into town to go home, he detoured to Mikey's. From the sidewalk he could see it was busy inside, and the warmth of the smoky bar was just what he wanted at the moment.

He walked in and stood for a moment, letting his eyes adjust to the dim light. He made his way to the bar and took the open stool, realizing a little too late that Millie Bing was on the stool beside him.

"Well, look who's here," she said loudly. "The man himself. Running for office. Going to be an elderman, huh?"

"Hi there, Millie. Nice to see you too."

"I can't believe you are running for office. Is there an age requirement for that job?"

"There is, and I meet it. Thank you very much for your confidence."

"Oh, I have confidence," Millie said.

Henry suspected she'd been at Mikey's a long time.

"I have the utmost confidence in your ability to be an elder. Elder man. Why not? You went to the Cities to get yourself educated and now you come back home to straighten us all out. Mr. Professor."

Henry tried to smile. The teasing was harsh and loud. He didn't want to feed it by reacting.

"Yup, you come home to roost. Got you a degree, no job, and lots of time on your hands—so you're gonna run for office. Fix the world. Change the town. Ladies and gents, let me introduce Hank Alexander, long lost resident of Copper Prairie, back from the Cities, finally come home."

"Uh, Millie, okay. Enough." Henry was getting uncomfortable with her show.

"Enough? I haven't had enough yet." She slouched over towards him sloppily, her eyes glazed and half shut, looking like she would either pass out or kiss him. He wanted neither. She leaned closer. He pressed her shoulders back gently.

"Millie, I think maybe you need to pack it in. I think you've had enough to drink."

"You think? The Professor thinks?"

"Yeah. I think."

She leaned towards him again, with that look of drunken lust.

"Come on, can I help you home?"

"You wanna take me home, elder Hank man? Shucks, that's awful nice of you. Gentle elder man. Sure. Let's go."

Henry knew this was a less than ideal situation. But getting her out of there before she did any real damage to his reputation, negligible though it was, was probably a good idea.

He helped her out to the sidewalk. She was in rough shape. But her focus on not falling over kept her from focusing on him too much. It was slow going, but he finally got her to her house two blocks off Oak Street.

"Want to come in, Hank? Have a nightcap or something?"

"No thanks, Millie. Maybe another time. It's been a long day. You get yourself to bed, now."

"Just what I was thinking . . . bed . . ."

"Go on. Good night, Millie. Good night."

Finally free of the woman, Henry went on back to his studio apartment. It took him a long time to fall asleep.

Chapter Eleven

Naomi Blue

With every gust of wind, the leaves were falling from the trees like rain. It seemed that fall was going to leap towards winter this year as the cold front from the northwest blew hard into the town of Copper Prairie. The maple leaves had fallen first, and now the oaks were finally giving in. The grass on Naomi Blue's yard was barely visible through the leaves. Could she leave them there all winter? Maybe the wind would blow the leaves down the tracks. Raking was inevitable, she realized.

She repeatedly threw an old weathered tennis ball across the yard for Beatrix. Although the dog seemed happiest lying wherever the sun shone, catching its rays in the front hall, in the empty dining room, or on the back porch in the late afternoon, she had boundless energy for a tennis ball. Naomi did not share that energy. She turned towards the shed. Beatrix, tennis ball in mouth, joined her.

"Maybe we can get in here, huh, Beatrix?" She shook the rusted padlock. "There must be a rake in here."

Beatrix dropped the ball and began sniffing intently at the foundation of the shed. Naomi examined the door more closely. There must be a way in there, she thought. She walked around the shed, unsuccessful in avoiding the burs that had gotten Beatrix the last time the dog had been sniffing back here. They caught in Naomi's socks, nipping at her ankles as she walked.

Naomi sat down on the back step to get the burs off, thinking that it was time to get into the shed. After all, it was her shed. Perhaps her friend at the police station might be able to help, that Officer Millerton.

When the call came into the police station that afternoon, Dan Millerton was the only one around. Officer Millerton's view of being a police officer in a small town meant he was the man for all jobs. He could answer phones, take notes, check the database for wanted felons, run licenses, make arrests, investigate stolen bicycles, open locked cars, and anything else that happened of concern in the town of Copper Prairie. He liked being the "go to" man in town. It was more than simply loving his job; he somehow was the job. There were slow times, however. In fact, most times were slow. Weekend nights were busy down at the Ringworm, and occasionally at Mikey's, but those who drank didn't usually have too far to go home, so if they kept their hands in their pockets and didn't rough each other up, it was quiet enough for Officer Millerton. Around homecoming at the Central School there was usually a spate of pranks, sometimes done by bored kids in the next town to the north, but nothing serious enough that he had any real job to do. He often got the calls, took notes in the pad he kept in his chest pocket, went out to "investigate" and then closed the case after listening and calming the complainer. After each "case," Officer Millerton would tear the note sheet off the pad carefully, and place it in a folder that was then filed chronologically in one of the large steel file cabinets in the back of the station.

He headed out to widow Wanda Cooper's old house where this Naomi Blue lived. It would always be the Coopers' house, Officer Millerton thought. It would take a long time to shift ownership in his mind. He remembered old man Cooper, a small quiet wiry man. He'd been a city elder for twenty-four years, until he died during a town zoning meeting. There had been a discussion about the sale of one of the town's last remaining farms that abutted the south side of Oak Street and whether it should be developed into a suburban style housing development, like the ones sprawling around the Cities. It had been a contentious meeting. The third and fourth generation families wanted Copper Prairie to retain its small town Midwest appeal, keeping the farms in the hands of families. But many of the younger residents had no need of local farms and wanted to move out of the "charming" houses in town with their neat front lawns, American flags angled out from the side of the front doors, and a shade-providing elm or oak on the front lawn. Modern new houses close to town were starting to emerge from soy acreage and cornfields. And during this discussion, right after Sebastian Skinner's halting speech with the microphone cutting out so that every fourth word he uttered was missing, and precisely during Rooster Robinson's plea for change as a way to increase the vitality of the business economy, just as he explained how slow things were in the grocery business, how he wanted the town to grow and prosper, Lyle Cooper put his head down on his chest and stopped breathing. No one had noticed. It was not uncommon for Lyle to take a catnap during a long meeting, especially one with his long time cronies coming up to speak one at a time, droning on too long for his patience. Lyle would normally wake up in time for a vote, or if someone mentioned his name, sputtering a bit, clearing his throat, and pretending that he hadn't been asleep.

But when the time had come for a roll call vote for the development, with the town hall crowded with residents and the developers standing along the far wall in black suits and once-crisp starched white shirts, Lyle Cooper had not voted. The mayor let out a deep ahem in his throat, closer to a gargle than anything, as if he needed to remove some offending substance. Officer Millerton had been beckoned. While a volunteer officer tried to clear the packed room, Officer Millerton checked for a pulse. Lyle Cooper was already cold to the touch by the time Dan Millerton placed his three fingers on the man's wrinkled neck. And although it was the first time that Officer Dan Millerton had touched a dead person, he turned to the city clerk and said calmly, "Now would be a good time to call Wanda."

The vote was recorded as three in favor, two opposed and one abstention. That week, Wanda Cooper buried her husband in the northeast corner of the cemetery on John Moore Road under a low, flowering crab apple tree, the branches so heavy with blossoms, the backhoe had trouble digging close to it. Her children fixed up the house, put it on the market, and Wanda moved south before the sold sign was hung. It had sat vacant for a long time before it finally sold far below market value to Naomi Blue.

And now Office Dan Millerton was headed out to the Cooper's house to see what Naomi Blue's shed issue was about. The last time he'd been to the house had been for a reception of sorts, immediately following the burial. Most of the younger members of the family had walked from the cemetery back to the house, in a long line of dark clothing that snaked from John Moore Road right into town. The small house had been crowded and hot, too many soft deep easy chairs and too many people. The dining room table was lined with three pans of Jell-O and an assortment of hot dishes. He had paid his respects to Wanda Cooper and left quickly. There were still people who would have preferred he left the uniform behind on calls like this. He saw them eyeing the holster, the heavy belt, and the thick-soled shiny shoes. But he wore it anyway.

When Naomi Blue opened the door for him, he was startled. He pretended not to notice really, to avoid her thinking him rude, but there was utterly nothing in the dining room except the chandelier and nothing at all in the living room.

"Hello, Ms. Blue. What is the problem with the shed?"

"Hi, Officer. Well, it's locked. And I didn't get a key when I moved in. I think there must be a key somewhere, but I can't find it. I've looked everywhere I could think, in all the kitchen drawers, the shelves, everywhere really. I was hoping you might be able to help me break in."

"Let's take a look."

They walked around to the back, Beatrix leading the way, excited for the visitor and to be outside. She found a tennis ball hidden in the leaves and brought it to the police officer.

"Not now, Beatrix," Naomi said.

Officer Millerton looked at the backyard that was so different now that the Coopers were gone. Unkempt. He hesitated before walking out to the shed. He wasn't keen on getting his shoes spotted from the damp leaves and who knew what else from the dog. But it was his job. He walked to the shed.

"It's locked all right," he said.

Naomi resisted the temptation to say something sarcastic. She waited politely.

"Well, I could open it with a bolt cutter for sure. Don't have one of those with me, though." The truth was, Officer Millerton had every tool imaginable in the back of the truck, but he did not like the idea of breaking into Lyle Cooper's old shed. It seemed a violation of sorts, an invasion of privacy. It just didn't seem right to break in. He knew this wasn't logical, even while he saw the world as a set of rules, of right and wrong, of logic and clarity. And surely this woman had a right to go into the shed. But he could not help her break in.

"I would suggest that you look further for the key before we do damage to the door or lock. I'm sure that key is somewhere. It would be better not to wreck the door."

"I'm sure it's somewhere too. But where?" Naomi was frustrated. She thought he'd come with a solution, but he seemed not interesting in helping.

"Have you looked everywhere?"

"I've looked all around the house. No key."

"Well, think about where a man would hide something, not where a woman would. If you still can't find the key, I'll come back with bolt cutters."

Officer Millerton got into his squad car and drove off, leaving Naomi Blue standing on the front step. Where would a man hide a key, she wondered. Not in the kitchen, she thought, not if you were trying to keep something private from your wife. But where?

Naomi renewed her search upstairs in her bedroom. She pulled the rickety chair over to the closet and balanced herself carefully to feel along the edges and corners of the high shelf; the heat from the bare light bulb threatened to burn her hand. No key. The chair felt suddenly wobbly and she held onto the shelf for balance. The chair was not up to the challenge and it didn't seem worth the effort. No key there anyway.

Naomi went down to the kitchen. This was an unlikely hiding place for a key. It was also probably Wanda Cooper's domain. And it was the one room on the first floor that Naomi actually used and had cleaned fastidiously when she moved in. Still, Naomi went through all the drawers again, pulling them out completely to peek behind and climbed up on the counters to check in all of the higher cabinets, above the cabinets and above the refrigerator. No key.

The dining room and living room were empty, but maybe he hid the key around the chandelier? Naomi knew this was getting ridiculous.

Nothing is this important. I don't want to rake the leaves anyway. The key will be found eventually and that will be soon enough for me, she decided.

Chapter Twelve

Henry Alexander

Election day was only eight days away and Henry was getting nervous. He had actually spent a fair number of afternoons walking through town shaking hands with people, wearing his green "Henry Morgan Alexander 4 City Elder" button, two buttons actually. He'd printed up 200 flyers that he handed out to anyone who seemed even remotely interested in the election. He sold himself as the "fresh face" running for city elder. He talked about how he'd lived there most of his life, how the vitality of the town was his priority, how he would listen to citizen concerns, and make things better for all. Henry talked fast and he talked well. He tried not to sound know-it-all or arrogant, two things his parents had harped on him for being most of his life. It didn't help that he did think he knew it all and that he was a bit arrogant. So he tried to sound smart, but not too smart. He wanted to seem like a regular guy. He spent equal amounts of time at the Ringworm and at Mikey's—and of course, at Ida's Bakery.

The one kiss he'd had with Naomi Blue had increased his interest in her, though an outside observer might call it something akin to an obsession. Whatever he did, wherever he went in Copper Prairie, he was aware of where she was. He only went to Ida's when she was there. He took walks hoping to run into her walking the dog. And he made sure that most of his routes took him by the Carriage General. Watching her in the window, still as a doll, was one of the most thrilling, and admittedly arousing, times of his week. He could stand and watch her for long periods of time. He was supposed to watch her, he reasoned, that's why she was standing in the window! To attract customers, like him.

Uncomfortably, Henry realized that he had not gone into the store since Naomi Blue began modeling, and that for her to keep the job, there probably had to be a resulting increase in business. And he did want her to keep the job, if not for her sake, at least for his. He promised himself that the next day he saw her modeling in the window, he would go in and shop.

That day came quickly. It was a miserably windy autumn day, the kind of day where the temperature doesn't tell the full story. The blustery wind made it feel thirty degrees, although it was really forty-two. He had a black cap on as he walked down Carriage Street. He wished he had on something warmer than a sweatshirt. He glanced at the window. She was there.

She was posed on a chair today, her legs crossed, right elbow resting on her thigh. She wore a crisp white shirt over black jeans. Spiky black heels. Her long hair was down around her face. She looked out over his head. Henry just stood there and stared. She didn't move. Did she know he was there? Did she see him there? She showed no recognition. Not a flicker or twitch. He stood until he began to shiver. Henry went inside.

"Hello," Henry said to the shopkeeper, a man he vaguely remembered. "It's nice to be out of that wind."

"Yes, I'm sure it is. It's gotten to be a lot like winter already. It's not even November."

Henry pulled his hands out of his pocket. "Hi, I'm Henry Alexander, and I'm running for city elder."

"You don't say? Well, I'm Sebastian Skinner. Nice to meet you."

"Same. I have this brochure describing my candidacy . . ." Henry handed him a flyer.

"Henry Morgan Alexander," the man said. "Henry Morgan Alexander. You wouldn't be John and Myrtle's boy, would you now?"

"Yes, I am. That's me. You know them?"

"Of course. Well, I did know them. Before they moved."

"They're out in Arizona now, where it's a bit warmer than this."

"That's right, I remember that now."

"How do you know them?"

"Your mother used to work here when she was in high school."

"No sh- I mean, no kidding?"

"No kidding. She came right from school four days a week."

"How do you know my dad?"

"He came here four days a week too, just to see her. I finally had to tell him that unless he bought something, he had to leave; he could not just hang out here watching her work."

"We're talking about my parents? I never heard this before."

"Well, they were indeed crazy about each other. Crazy in love. Caught them in the back storage room one night, even. Ooh hoo, that was a bad night for them. They had a choice—my lecture and an afternoon of unpaid work or I told their parents. They took my lecture. Fooling around in the back room, that was a first."

"My parents?"

"You're John and Myrtle's boy, right?"

"Yes."

"Well, that was them."

"Wow." Henry didn't like to imagine his parents fooling around, and particularly not fooling around in the back room of the Carriage General. It was a strange thought. He glanced back towards the front of the store, where Naomi Blue sat teasingly in the window.

To dispel the image of his parents, and the even more interesting one of Naomi Blue, Henry began to browse through the store. The men's clothing was not what you might find in the Twin

Cities. It was a kind of classic northern style: useful flannel-lined shirts, Carhartt coveralls and jackets, wool socks, embossed leather belts, work boots and other clothing that could just as likely have been sold forty years earlier when his mother worked there.

"Son, you know I've got an upstairs with household goods and such," Sebastian Skinner said. "All sorts of things you can't live without."

Eager to be a good customer, Henry dutifully went up the stairs in the back of the store, wooden steps worn and concave from years of walking on. The upstairs was filled, completely crowded, with place mats, area rugs, hand mixers, coffee makers, towels, hoses, mops, muffin tins, hammers, clocks, suitcases, lamps, and an oddly bright display of toilet brushes in seven rainbow colors. Henry could barely walk without brushing up against another display or stack of merchandise. The Carriage General seemed to have everything, including dust. How long had all this stuff been up there, Henry wondered.

Henry felt a compulsion to wander slowly though the clutter, like a kid on a treasure hunt, hoping to find something that had been long forgotten. He laughed to himself. Maybe everything was long forgotten. He might just find something valuable though. He had the same feeling in antique shops, that there was a treasure somewhere, if only he could find it. And then something caught his eye on the floor, surrounded by a fantastic number of multicolored woven decorative baskets. It was a wrought iron birdcage. It looked as if it might have once been white, but was now dusty and paint-chipped. It was his. He climbed into the mass of baskets, moving them into new piles and balancing them carefully on top of each other until he could get to the birdcage without causing a collapse. He lifted it up by its handle and brought it out to look at it more closely.

"Mr. Skinner," Henry said as he walked down the stairs. "I found the coolest thing for my apartment. This birdcage."

Sebastian Skinner was standing at the bottom of the stairs.

"Hello. How are you, young man? Can I help you?"

"Me? Fine. I, uh, I was just shopping upstairs," Henry said, realizing that Sebastian Skinner had something of a short memory.

"Oh. Yes."

"I found this birdcage. But I don't see a price on it."

"Let me take a look . . ."

Sebastian Skinner pulled out a pair of dirty half glasses and, after a few minutes of turning the cage on its side and around and peering within, he declared there was no price tag.

"What about fifteen dollars? Does that seem like a fair price?"

Henry had no idea if it was or not, and was happy to pay it. Henry walked out of the store with the birdcage in hand. He turned back to the window.

The chair was empty and Naomi Blue was gone; the manikin stood posing with her hand on her hip.

As he walked down the street, he began to feel foolish with the birdcage. What the hell was he going to do with a birdcage? With every step he took, it banged his leg. He began to wonder what had possessed him upstairs at the Carriage General to buy a birdcage. A birdcage? It was probably Naomi Blue's fault, he thought, *she distracts me, she makes me crazy.*

Perhaps Naomi Blue would like this birdcage, he wondered. Maybe it would be a nice decoration for her house. And that would give him an excuse to visit her.

SEBASTIAN SKINNER

JOHN AND MYRTLE'S BOY, SEBASTIAN MUSED. He did seem to resemble his father. John had been a fair skinned boy with a grand amount of blond hair that seemed too much for his head. He wore the same clothes every day, Sebastian recalled, those dirty jeans, t-shirt and jean jacket. Like a uniform. And every day chasing after Myrtle. She was a smart girl, smarter than most, and certainly smarter than John. He wouldn't have hired the boy under any circumstances, but the girl could balance the register drawer like nobody else, and she was friendly to the customers. That boy sure hung around too often. He used to wonder what Myrtle had seen in the boy. Myrtle herself had smarts but not much in the way of looks. Each of her features was just fine alone, but when they were put together on her face, well, it came up short, at least for Sebastian's taste. But clearly they loved each other. The day he'd happened upon them was not a pleasant memory. He had heard a strange sound in the back storage room, and it had not occurred to him what might be going on. He had opened the door abruptly and seen the half naked Myrtle with the completely naked John, so engrossed he didn't hear the door open. Myrtle had screamed and tried to cover herself. Sebastian was stunned and stood frozen, his hand still on the doorknob. When he regained his ability to move, he shut the door quickly. Right there, they'd been doing it. It was too much for him. Anger with a hint of envy—that was only partially defused by amusement—overtook him.

And they had emerged sheepishly, both of them, although it was John who wouldn't make eye contact. Myrtle looked at him a bit defiantly, knowing he wouldn't fire her. And he didn't. But he had lectured them and gotten hours of free work from them.

This boy Henry had his father's build but his mother's look of determination.

Naomi Blue

Meanwhile, Naomi was not far ahead of Henry on the walk to her house. She had left only minutes before him, having earned a beautiful blue and rust colored wool cap for her work. Surely she'd have warm clothes by winter if she kept modeling.

Modeling was a very odd experience. People did gather to watch. She could see them talking to each other. The window was well insulated so she couldn't hear anything, but she saw their animated faces. It was disconcerting. Most of the time, she didn't know the people on the street. Although one day Millie Bing had walked by and had frantically waved at her, with so much energy that she had to make eye contact. Millie smiled and gestured with her hand that Naomi should call. Naomi nodded ever so slightly at her and then fixed her eyes back on the bank awning.

Henry Alexander, however, was a regular. He would walk up slowly and stop, and stay there, staring at her. She could tell it was Henry without looking, by the bright green campaign buttons he wore on his jacket, and by the way he stood there, just stood there. Modeling was a true test. To ignore Henry was the hardest part about modeling. Not only because Henry had kissed her, but because Henry had *really* kissed her. And there he would be again. Sometimes he stood close up on the sidewalk and sometimes he stood across the street. She shivered. It was unnerving, really.

Naomi went in the house and let Beatrix out the back. The dog crouched quickly and followed Naomi back in the house. She was startled to hear knocking at the front. Beatrix ran barking ahead.

"Henry? Hi."

"Naomi. I, uh, hi."

Naomi started to ask him if he was campaigning when she saw that he was holding a rather large cage.

"What the heck is that?"

"A birdcage."

"Yes, I see that. Is it part of your door knocking for city elder? Maybe a platform of 'get rid of the old birds?'" Naomi couldn't resist teasing him.

Henry was clearly startled. He looked down at the rusty cage. "Well, I hadn't thought of that. Nice theme. Sort of. The birdcage was just so neat, I thought you might like it. For decoration or something."

Naomi was the one startled now. Such an odd gift. She took the birdcage that Henry was now holding out towards her. "Oh, nice . . ." As she turned to bring it into the house, she noticed that Henry had stepped up and was following her in.

"Come in, I guess, Henry. There's not much to see. And the bird cage will make a wonderful addition to my decor." Naomi Blue felt that perhaps humor would get her over the embarrassment of having no furniture. The birdcage might be an improvement.

Naomi heard Henry's footsteps stop behind her, and knew he was looking around at the house—the very empty house.

"It's a nice house. How long have you lived here?"

"Long enough to get furniture, I suppose. I will, eventually. Just saving up some money." She set the birdcage down in the dining room directly under the chandelier. They both stood back and admired it.

"It's nice, Henry. Thanks."

"I found it upstairs at the Carriage General. I thought it was really cool. I just thought you might like it."

"I do," Naomi said, not entirely with conviction. She did like the birdcage, but it was a strange gift and looked out of place in the empty room. "Maybe it would look better in the kitchen." Henry carried it to the kitchen. Naomi climbed on a chair and brought down the hanging spider plant from a hook in the corner. Henry handed her the birdcage and she lifted it onto the ceiling hook.

"What do you think?" she asked Henry.

"I like it there. Maybe you need a bird."

"I don't know about that. But maybe."

"Nice yard," Henry remarked, looking out the back kitchen door.

Naomi Blue opened the door, with Beatrix barely waiting for the screen door to open to rush outside.

"Really nice yard, Naomi. But you need to do some serious raking."

"I know. I was hoping to use wind power."

"Nah, that never works. I'd be happy to help you rake."

"That would be nice, but therein lies the problem. A rake. I don't have one. I'm thinking there must be one in the shed, but I can't find the key."

Henry went over to the shed and jiggled the padlock.

"I see. But it must be around here somewhere."

"I know. I've looked."

"Ah."

"Henry, so how come you keep going down to the Carriage General to watch me in the window?"

Henry wasn't quick to answer. He shuffled his feet through the leaves.

"You sure do have a lot of leaves." He thought deflection a good option.

Naomi laughed.

"Great backyard. The tracks are pretty close to the house though."

Naomi laughed again.

"Cute little birdhouse in this crab tree."

Naomi looked at the tree as if for the first time. A cute little birdhouse? The birdhouse. That might be a good place to hide a shed key. It was the perfect hiding place. It would have been handy for Mr. Cooper and yet not easily found by Wanda or anyone else. Naomi did not want to share this idea with Henry. This was something she would do on her own.

"So why do you watch me model?"

"I don't know. I just like it. I like to watch you. It's, I don't know, fun. Not fun. It's, I, uh, I'm not making any sense, am I?"

Naomi laughed. She liked seeing Henry awkward. It made her feel more comfortable.

"I like to watch you. I get to watch you while you're not watching me. There's something great about that. I admit it. I like to look at you."

Now Naomi was embarrassed. Neither of them knew what to say. Thankfully, Beatrix came up with a tennis ball and pressed it against Henry's thigh. He tossed it across the yard repeatedly. The dog didn't let up. Meanwhile, Naomi regained her composure.

"Henry. Thanks again for the birdcage. I like it."

"Naomi, I like you."

That's all it took for Naomi to feel ill at ease again.

"I mean, well, Naomi, ever since I kissed you, I think you've been avoiding me."

"I haven't been avoiding you, but Henry, there is one thing. One problem. It's awkward to talk about. But I am older than you. A lot older."

"So what?"

"So it matters."

"Why? It doesn't matter to me. Did it matter when I kissed you the other day?"

Naomi felt once again the effect the single kiss had had on her. She was silent.

"Naomi . . ." She heard the sound in his voice, the particular way he said her name, and she knew he wanted her. She didn't know what to say.

"Naomi, forget about our ages. I might be a city elder next week." As Naomi laughed, he pulled her towards him and kissed her. Just like the first kiss. Except this time, she put her arms around him as well.

Naomi's resistance dropped completely. All the effort she had given towards pretending she wasn't interested in Henry had given rise to a lustful sort of energy. If he was too young, it no longer mattered enough to stop the events that inevitably followed. She led him into the house, and up the narrow staircase to her room, with Beatrix bounding up behind them. As Henry slowly undressed her, murmuring about her skin, her softness, she lost the self-consciousness of the years between them. She closed her eyes as all the truths which she was certain were visible on her skin were revealed. Henry tossed his clothes to the floor and then came beside her on the bed. She opened her eyes to look at him. As he traced around her eyes with the tip of his finger, down the side of her cheek, continuing on to her neck, and then to her breast, she closed her eyes and shivered. The last thing on her mind was his age.

The afternoon turned into early autumn darkness, and the night freight train rumbled by right on time.

IDA MINSKY

WHY NOT EXPECT THE GIRL TO BE ON TIME. *Is that too much to ask? One girl living alone in a house with nothing but a mutt and she can't be on time? I don't think I'm asking too much, no, not too much. Seven o'clock is not too early. Ach, I've been up since before dawn and I stayed up late. If I am here, she can be here. She can get here by seven. Is that too much to ask?*

She pulled the cakes out of the oven and set them aside to cool. She was behind her normal schedule and had not yet finished kneading the dough for the rolls. The hot ovens sat empty. She had an unusual amount of strength this morning for the dough. She used her knuckles and turned it and then again. This was the reason her bread was so good, yes, it was the kneading by hand. Nothing could compete with the hands of a woman. No machine could knead with the passion and force of an emotional woman.

The door jangled open. Ida kept on kneading.

"Ida? I'm here," the girl called tentatively. "I'm so sorry I'm late. Not too late, only fifteen minutes. Ida?"

Ida stood in the kitchen doorway, hands on her hips, watching the girl take off her wool sweater and hat.

"Eighteen minutes. You're eighteen minutes late."

Naomi Blue glanced up at the clock. Eighteen minutes late.

"I'm really sorry. I can stay late today, or skip my break, or whatever you want, Mrs. Minsky." She tossed her sweater under the counter and washed her hands. She was a good girl, really, not a problem. But Ida didn't want to be easy on her, no that wouldn't do, because then she might take advantage, and she couldn't have that.

"It smells great in here," Naomi Blue said, peeking in the back to see what was fresh out of the oven. While Ida Minsky continued with her rolls, Naomi put each cake on a cardboard round covered with a doily. She slid the cakes into the front display. She measured out the coffee and set it to brew. No customers. All was well.

When the rolls were finally in the oven, and eight customers had come in and out in a flurry, Ida came out beside the girl.

"So what was so important that you were late? May I ask that?"

"Uh, I had a hard time getting up this morning. That's all."

"Oh? Did you stay up too late?" The girl looked different today. Flushed. No eye contact. Something was different. She was certain something was different.

"Kind of."

"Yes, I see." Ida only thought she saw. Was the girl out at the Ringworm with the rest of the young folks in town? Was she drinking now? Was she with a man? Ah, maybe. Ida thought Naomi must have been with a man because when you're falling in love yourself, you think everyone is falling in love. More mportantly, when you spend the night up late with a man, you see that everywhere too. The one thing Ida Minsky was sure of, however, was that Naomi Blue was eighteen minutes late. And, of course, that Rooster Robinson had been in her own bed.

What do you call a man friend when you're my age, she wondered. *Rooster Robinson is my boyfriend,* she tried out in her mind. *Ach, no. That's ridiculous. Women my age don't have boyfriends. He's my lover. No, that implies just sex. Partner? Not right, he is not that. Beau? Yes, now that was about right. I'd like you to meet my beau, Roger. That had a funny ring to it.* Like a schoolgirl, she played with the possibilities.

Rooster Robinson was now a regular at Ida's Bakery. She knew what days he'd come because she knew what he most liked. Tuesday's pecan rings were his favorite, followed by Thursday's fruit tarts—berries or apples, he didn't care. Today was Tuesday and he would be here before ten o'clock.

Rooster was also a regular at her back door. She would see him coming from her chair in the window. This arrangement required her to stay up a bit later than normal and if she wasn't careful, she would fall asleep in the chair. So shortly before the prearranged time, Ida would get up and make sure she was presentable, rebraid her hair and brush her teeth.

Sometimes Rooster came for supper. He would carry a sack full of groceries from his store and Ida would unpack them on the counter and decide what to make. He seemed to find her cooking wonderful, if only for the fact that someone was cooking for him. She cooked him hot meals, seasoned with spices he didn't often eat, meals that Ida served to him with a sense of formality. Ida never knew what ingredients he would bring. The man surely didn't know any recipes, but he would reliably bring two types of vegetables, some sort of meat and nearly always potatoes. Russet potatoes, Yukon Golds, new potatoes, fingerling potatoes—each day different than the day before. Ida took Rooster's food choices as a cooking challenge. Rooster was grateful, almost too much so, as she brought the plates to the table. He complimented her cooking talents, thanked her for her efforts, and ate like a man who hadn't eaten in days.

They had much in common, as it turned out, particularly their immigrant families and old world stories. Their families were from different countries and their habits equally dissimilar, but they both viewed the world in context of the importance of hard work and the challenges their parents had encountered raising them as Americans. They often talked about the customers they shared in the town of Copper Prairie. They compared notes on who bought what, who were the difficult customers, what the new gossip was, who was ill, whose child had moved to the Twin Cities, and any irrelevant and irreverent detail that had been shared with them.

She let Roger stay overnight. While there was a comfort in having him stay, it had been so many years since she had shared any part of her life with a man. And it had been even more years since she had shared her bed. In the darkness of her apartment, with the shades drawn tight and even the light from her glowing clock turned towards the wall, Ida let this man see her body. There was a bit of comfort, but only a bit, in the fact that his body matched hers in age and softness. He didn't seem to care. His hands roamed across her skin finding what they wanted. Tentatively, so did she.

At 4:45 a.m., as her alarm went off, she nudged Roger to get him up. She wanted her secrets. She wanted her morning routine to be her own. She wanted him gone by daylight. He grumbled as he pulled on his pants and found his shoes in the hall closet. He left quickly with few words spoken. But not before he kissed her briefly on her cheek.

"Ida?" Naomi Blue said. "You look like you're thinking about something serious. You okay? I think you look like the tired one here."

Ida had been lost in her thoughts. Rooster Robinson had taken up residence in her mind.

"I am tired too, Naomi. I haven't been sleeping well."

"Dreams? Bad dreams?"

"Not exactly. Not exactly."

Chapter Thirteen

Naomi Blue

When Naomi Blue got off work, there was still a little bit of daylight. She rushed home determined to see if the birdhouse out back might really hold the key. The more she thought about it, the more certain she was that Lyle Cooper had hidden his padlock key there. She let Beatrix out the back and took the kitchen stepladder out to the tree. The birdhouse would not come down. Its wire moorings had been twisted around the branch so long ago that the wire was partially embedded into the branch. With one eye she peered in the round birdhouse door. It was impossible to see anything. She cautiously stuck her finger in and moved it around. Dried grass. She carefully began to pull out the nesting material. Feathers, grass, bits of dog fur, pieces of leaves and other unidentifiable matter came out in clumps as she did her best to get two fingers in the hole. Finally she was able to shake it.

A key fell to the ground. Naomi knew it. She knew it was in there. She dug the key out of the leaves where it had fallen. Finally she had the key. She went over to the shed door with a sudden feeling of apprehension as she stuck the key in the padlock. The arm swung away. She slipped the padlock off the door and put it into her pocket. The door seemed stuck in place. With some effort, Naomi pulled open the door.

The late afternoon light filtered in the doorway. The shed did not have a rake or a shovel. Nor did it have any other sort of tool. Every inch of wall space was covered with birdhouses. An assortment of birdhouses. No two identical. There was a narrow pine birdhouse next to an oak mansion of a birdhouse. Some were made of old barn wood, red and weathered. One had asphalt roof tiles on top. Quite a few were made from old fences. They were made of every imaginable kind of wood. Scraps. Weathered wood. There was a large martin house next to a small-holed bluebird house. Some of the houses were fanciful versions of real houses. There were Cape Cods, Victorian and Colonials. There was hardly an inch of wall space not covered by a birdhouse. And in the center of the shed, set right in the middle, was a rocking chair.

Naomi Blue stepped into the shed, letting her eyes adjust to the dimness. There was a faint musty smell. Cautiously, she stepped over to the back wall. The birdhouses were attached to the walls like a mosaic, fitting together as if he had built one house to nestle in next to the house beside it. She looked for a light switch next to the door. No switch, but there were a few things hung on nails. A hammer. A spool of wire. Wire cutters. On the other side of the door was a small wooden shelf with a pad of paper, a few carpenter pencils and a dusty blue box of 2" nails.

This was not a shed. Nor was it a workshop, Naomi realized. There was hardly any room in it. It was really just big enough for the birdhouses and the chair. She stepped carefully around the shed looking at the houses while Beatrix waited outside, her ears alert. Naomi was baffled. Why would someone have a shed for birdhouses? Why would anyone build so many birdhouses?

She sat on the rocking chair facing towards the door. Beatrix gave out a whimper. "Come on girl, you can come in." Beatrix stood up and edged closer to the shed, sniffing it cautiously. She put her front paws inside and looked up at Naomi.

"Good girl." But Beatrix backed up to wait outside. Naomi turned the chair around to face away from the door and rocked back in the chair, silent on the dirt floor. Beatrix barked. Naomi got up slowly. There was something so odd about this. Unnerved, Naomi got up.

She locked the shed and brought the key inside. The birdhouse out in the tree was too hard to get to. She dropped it into the bottom of the birdcage.

Why birdhouses? Why lock them into a shed and hide the key? Why hide the birdhouses at all?

Henry Alexander

Henry did like hanging out at Mikey's in the evenings. It wasn't the ambience exactly that he liked, but the being part of something in the community. Despite the fact that this was not exactly the involvement he was hoping for since he really needed a job, it kept him social and he liked that. Besides, he reasoned, this was all a part of running for office. Talk to the community, find out what mattered to them, and most of all, listen. Then get elected. He kept a handful of flyers in his coat pocket, and freely handed them out at the bar. He had better luck at Mikey's than at the Ringworm. The crowd was a little rougher down the street. Some of the guys teased him when he talked about becoming a city elder, and didn't really want a brochure, laughing as they said, "No thanks, but what about a beer?" The women seemed more interested, maybe only amused, but they listened to him talk about his campaign and promised they'd vote for him. If only they would.

He was sitting at the bar when a short stocky older man came up to the bar, turning sideways to slide between the stools and settle down upon one. He bumped Henry as he did so.

"Excuse me," the man said to Henry.

"Not a problem." Henry continued to look down at his beer. The man started to talk. Apparently to him.

"Winter is nearly here, yah, it's getting mighty cold out there. Cold for November, don't you think?" And then to the bartender, "A Sam Adams, please, if you would."

Henry glanced at the man to see who he was talking to.

"Yeah, it is cold. Not much of a fall either. The trees seemed so dull this year, didn't they?" Henry responded.

"Yup, sure did."

"Well, I hope this cold weather doesn't keep anyone from the polls on Election Day."

The man turned to him with an odd look, as if to see if Henry was kidding. "Election Day?"

"Yes," Henry replied. "I'm running for city elder. My name is Henry Morgan Alexander."

"Henry Morgan Alexander? That sure is a long name for someone your age. You really running for city elder?"

"Yes, I am. And yeah, it is a long name."

"Well, I'm Rooster Robinson," and he held out his hand. The man's stocky strong fingers rigorously gripped Henry's hand and he had work to avoid visibly wincing.

"Rooster Robinson? As in the grocery store Robinson?"

"Yup, that's me."

"Ah, okay. Pleased to meet you, Mr. Robinson."

"Call me Rooster."

"Okay. Will do."

"Why the hell are you running for city elder? I don't think we've ever had anyone under the age of seventy run for city elder."

"I wanted to do something good for the town, give back, serve the people, make change. It never occurred to me that I was too young."

"Well, they don't call it city elder for nothing."

Henry wasn't sure if he were being teased or if his age was a genuine problem. Was he really too young to be city elder and also too young to make love to Naomi Blue? Henry wondered why everyone seemed to be hung up on his age.

"Mr. Robinson, er, Rooster, I think it's a good thing to have fresh thinking on the city council. It can't hurt, really. I am open-minded and receptive to the community. Gray hair isn't the only determining factor of a good city elder."

"Ah, Henry, ease up, son. I'm just teasing you. You seem genuine enough. I'll vote for you, sure I will. I think you can't be worse than the old men on there now. At least you won't fall asleep during meetings!" And he started laughing. Henry started to laugh as well but wasn't sure why that was so funny. But the more he held it in, the more it backed up, until beer was coming out his nose. Rooster, already laughing, saw the beer spurting from Henry's nose and laughed without restraint, causing people to turn to see what the commotion was. By this time, Henry and Rooster were both laughing so hard, it no longer mattered what was or was not funny.

Political allies, as well as friendship, sometimes grow from long nights in places like Mikey's. Henry and Rooster stayed until the two o'clock in the morning closing time.

IDA MINSKY

NOVEMBER WINDS BLEW THROUGH Copper Prairie. The trees had finally given up their leaves, even those old oaks that seemed to hold on until snow was on the ground. Ida had barely noticed fall, to be honest. She had not seen the leaves turn golden and clutter the yards. If it weren't for the influx of tourists who travel north to bear witness to the turning season and the resultant increase in sales, she might not have noticed it at all. She was off balance in exactly the way people who have been on their own for many years become off balance when another person becomes a part of their lives. She recognized it as both wonderful and terribly annoying. Long ago she had vowed that relationships with men were something she did not need. And yet as Rooster Robinson had become concerned with her wellbeing, grateful for her attentions, and a devoted companion in bed, she relented her steadfast independence.

She had not spoken of this relationship to anybody yet. It felt easier to keep it a secret, though she realized that secrets like this could give rise to the most energetic gossip in town. But until that time, she was safe in her privacy. And who to tell anyway? Ida was not particularly social. She kept hours that weren't conducive to much socializing. Oh, there were the regular customers that came in and chatted. And she attended the Prairie Thanksgiving Festival the town held in the Copper Prarie Central School gym in November, bringing a dessert to put on the long buffet table. She also had a small booth in late July at the Copper Crafts Show, held on the football field of the high school. It was a wonderful display of local jams, quilts, wooden toys, baked goods, knitted hats and scarves, bird houses, woodcut prints of moose, bear and evergreen trees, and whatever else anyone created. Tourists came up north to shop and the town buzzed with the air of "chic" despite the fact that most of the time, it was a quiet unimaginative place to be. Ida would close the bakery and sell her baked goods from a long folding table covered with a red and white checked plastic tablecloth. She would chat with people as they walked slowly around the booths.

But divulging secrets was another matter. There was her employee, of course, Naomi Blue. Young enough to be her daughter, or perhaps even a granddaughter, how could she confide in her? What would she know about love? A girl like Naomi, living alone in such a small town, walking about without a coat on frigid mornings—what kind of confidant would she be? And the rumor she had heard about the girl. Ah, no rumor, no rumor, she was sure it was no rumor. She'd heard that the girl was pretending to be a manikin in the Carriage General window. That she stood absolutely still in the window, next to the real manikin. That she looked into nothingness, as if she wasn't real. All dolled up in boots and skirts and fancy clothes, at least as fancy as what Sebastian had in the place. She bet Sebastian loved this arrangement. Naomi Blue did not look much like a model to Ida. Not like a model at all. She was a simple sort of pretty, Ida supposed, though no great beauty. She was curvier than models normally were—too buxom, too full, too much. So am I, so am I, thought Ida, but at least I don't model.

Perhaps giving voice to her relationship with Roger would be a poor choice. It would make it all the more real.

Chapter Fourteen

Naomi Blue

Naomi stood in the kitchen, looking out the window. It was so cold in there that her coffee was chilling faster than she could drink it. She stared out at the shed. She had stood at the window precisely like this every morning for the past few days. She looked at the single birdhouse hanging from the tree, wondering.

Finally, she opened the birdcage and took out the key. She went out the back door. The overnight frost left a crisp whiteness on the leaves on the grass. She unlocked the shed. She stood there for a moment letting the fresh air mix into the stale air of the shed, and to let any mice that might be nesting inside scurry out before she stepped in. She wasn't fond of mice. She lifted the rocking chair and brought it outside on the grass. Naomi hadn't really looked at the chair before, couldn't really, because of the lack of light in the shed. It was unusual, unlike any rocking chair she'd ever seen. The rocking chair seat was inlaid wood, all different shades. She recognized oak and maple, perhaps even walnut, but she wasn't sure. It was beautiful. The back slats were a solid piece of wood in alternating colors. She had never seen a chair like it.

She carried it carefully into the house. As she angled it in the door, she noticed something on the bottom of the chair, a tag of some sort. She tipped the chair over and crouched down to read it. It was a bit of leather tacked into the underside of the chair. A shaky hand had written in ink:

> "Hand made by Lyle Cooper in the year of our Lord nineteen hundred forty-eight. Crafted from birch, oak, maple, walnut, beech and elm. No screws or nails have been used in this creation. Hidden within each tree is the marvel of time.
> Lyle Cooper
> Copper Prairie, Minnesota, USA"

How odd, Naomi thought. In the storage shed was the finest piece of furniture she had ever seen. It was definitely the finest piece of furniture Naomi Blue had ever owned. But the birdhouses…that was just strange. Why was this amazing chair in the shed? Did he just sit in there and think? Look at the birdhouses? What? Shaking her head, Naomi looked at the chair. Now she finally had a piece of furniture for her house. She put it into the living room, facing in towards the center of the room. It looked awkward with nothing else there at all. She turned it around to face the window, sat down and rocked.

She might have dozed off, she wasn't sure. But the ringing phone startled her into alertness.

"Hey, Naomi, this is Millie. Millie Bing."

Millie Bing. Naomi Blue suddenly remembered Millie standing outside the Carriage General gesturing that she would call.

"Hi Millie. How are you?"

"Great, come on, let's go get a burger at the Ringworm. You're not a vegetarian, are you?"

"Uh, no…"

"Good, so meet me? It'd be fun to catch up."

Naomi Blue agreed to an early supper at the Ringworm. Their burgers were famed to be the best in Copper Prairie, although there wasn't too much competition. As Naomi walked down to the bar, she thought about the circle of friends that she was finally developing. It was slow, but she was beginning to feel a part of Copper Prairie. Maybe Millie would turn into a good friend, a real girl friend, someone she could talk about stuff with, or even talk to about Henry. She picked up her pace with the good feeling that came from this new positive attitude as well as the desire to get out of the wind a little sooner.

The Ringworm was still relatively quiet when she got there. Millie was at the bar already, a beer half finished. She sat down on the stool beside her.

"Hey, you're here," Millie said. "Let's grab a table."

They took a small round table in the front window where the early dusk light still brightened the street.

Over burgers and beers they seemed old friends. Naomi, despite her eagerness for friendship, was something of a reluctant friend. She wanted the connection but was uncomfortable with the intimacy of friendship. Millie talked a lot. In fact, Millie talked too much. But it was safer than being asked too many questions, so Naomi munched on her chips and let the conversation flow in whatever direction Millie took it.

"Anything new in your love life, Naomi?"

Naomi coughed on the potato chip.

"New in my love life? What love life?"

Millie laughed. "Yeah, I know what you mean. Not much going on here either. But I do have a crush on a guy."

"A crush? Who is he?"

"Oh, he's a guy I used to know in high school. He's pretty cute. Moved back to town this year. I hadn't seen him in years, but now he's back."

"Oh."

"Yeah, well, we've had a couple of drinks together. We're still getting reacquainted, I guess you could say."

"That sounds okay. What's his name?"

"Hank. Hank Alexander."

"As in Henry Alexander?"

"Yeah, that's the name he's using in politics. He's running for city elder. Maybe you've seen his flyers."

"Uh, yes, I've seen his flyers. His name is really Hank?"

"That's what I've always called him."

"Oh. So you're dating him?" Naomi was getting uncomfortable. Uneasy. Perhaps even a little jealous. She wasn't sure. She just felt the need for more details.

"Well, I wouldn't actually say I'm dating him. But I do have a thing for him. I think he might be interested in me. Took me home one night. I would love to make it more. He's really something. He's smart and funny, very cute."

Naomi wasn't sure what to say. She had wanted to tell Millie about her relationship with Henry. Hank. But now it didn't seem right. It didn't seem possible. Not when Millie was interested in him. Not if they went out together. And even without Millie's own interest in Henry, what would Millie even think of her and Henry together with more than a decade separating them? She felt old.

It was dark before Naomi Blue left the Ringworm. It had begun to get crowded and Millie had begun to get drunk. Millie didn't leave when Naomi left. They had gotten up together, but Millie stopped at the bar to talk to the bartender and Naomi had gone out into the night without her. She walked home without the liveliness she had felt earlier. She slept deeply and darkly.

Henry Alexander

It was Monday. One day until Election Day. Henry was nervous. It made him nervous to think that he might win this election. The thought of losing was not too bad, but it would mean that he'd have to give more thought to what he was going to do, really do, with his life. Being a city elder was a distraction of sorts, and had been all fall. He knew that. But it was the sort of distraction that he had allowed because becoming a city elder was a good thing to do. And now it was potentially only a day away.

His campaign had gone well, although he hadn't done too much. He'd gone to most of the downtown businesses to introduce himself. He'd handed out flyers in Mikey's and the Ringworm, undoubtedly the oddest places to campaign. But it seemed that most of the town went to one or the other for drinks, food, or music. He felt he'd done a lot in comparison to the other candidates who had not done particularly anything to campaign—no doorknocking, no yard signs, no bar visits. There had been a series of quarter-page ads on page five of the *Copper Press* the week before last for a few candidates, one proclaiming "Experience, Dedication, Devotion." Another candidate's ad was a list of maybe 200 names of supporters in the community. And the third ad showed a large photo of the candidate sitting on his Bobcat, a trucker's cap shading his eyes and the words underneath the photo said, "I get the job done." There were five candidates for three open seats. One of the candidates was an incumbent, and Henry figured he had a good chance of being reelected. That left four of them vying for two seats. A fifty-fifty chance of being elected wasn't too bad. He had not met any of them yet. Last Friday's issue of the *Copper Press* had been devoted to the election. Each candidate had submitted their responses to a set of questions entitled "Elder Survey." Their responses had been printed alongside small photos of each of them in the paper. It was hard to predict what might happen. Just looking at the *Copper Press* highlighted quite a few distinctions between Henry and his competition, the most obvious of which was his age.

Henry wanted to shake off the nervous feeling the upcoming election brought. He thought he'd go visit Naomi at the bakery. She would be a good person to see at the moment, he thought.

He sensed it as soon as he walked into Ida's Bakery. He sensed it even before the bells stopped jangling and the door shut behind him. He knew something was different with Naomi when she turned her back on the door, even though Henry knew she'd seen him coming. Something was not as it had been. He walked up to the counter, looking at the white straps of the apron pressing into Naomi's waist. He wanted to hold her waist.

"Hi Naomi," Henry said tentatively. "Hi."

She turned around deliberately. "Can I get you something?"

Henry tipped his head to the side and looked curiously into her eyes.

"Yes." He smiled.

"Okay, what would you like?"

She was not teasing him. She was so even-toned. So devoid of emotion. Flat.

"I'd like to have a cup of coffee, please."

She went about getting his coffee ready, adding the cream and sugar just as he liked it.

"Here you go."

"Naomi…"

She looked up at him.

"Naomi, what's up?"

"What do you mean?"

"I mean, why are you acting like you don't know me. Is it because…"—and here he whispered—"because Ida is listening?"

"No."

"Well, what's wrong? You seem angry at me or something."

"No, I'm not angry. Can I get you anything else?"

"Yes."

"Yes?"

"Let's go for a walk later."

Naomi Blue didn't say anything. Henry paid for his coffee and went to sit at a table. Something was definitely wrong. She wasn't talking. He sipped his coffee, looking out the window. He wasn't sure if he had done something or not. He replayed the last time they'd been together. They had had an unbelievable night at her house. She had been loving, giving, physical and they had barely slept for more than a few hours. Even during those few hours he was only in a light sleep, aware of her presence every minute of the night. It had been quite a night. And he hadn't thought of much else since. She had such boundaries, more than most women he'd known, and he had tried to respect them. But in bed she had let those boundaries go, and she had been more talkative and open than he had seen before. It was almost a transformation, he thought. He had left early in the morning, when she got up to let the dog outside. She was a little distant in the morning, hard to read. But he had been certain about what had happened that night and about the connection between them. He had wondered if she wasn't a morning person. He'd been tentative with her, and had hugged her before he left, telling her that he would talk to her later. But neither of them had called the other. Maybe she was hurt.

Henry walked up to the counter with his empty coffee mug.
"I meant to call you."
"Oh, that's okay."
"Are you angry?"
"No," she replied.
"What are you then?"
"Working."
"Yes, but, what's up?"
"How about we talk later," Naomi said.
"Okay. Later."
Henry left without looking back. At least she was willing to talk.

IDA MINSKY

IDA DIDN'T THINK OF HERSELF AS AN EAVESDROPPER. No, that wasn't the right word for her. But she consistently and intently listened to the conversations that Naomi Blue had with customers. It wasn't actually eavesdropping or even inappropriate because it was Ida's store and Ida's customers. And if she didn't listen, she couldn't be sure that the girl's customer service was up to snuff. This morning, however, Ida felt that she was listening to a lovers' spat. Or it would be a spat if Naomi had really spoken. She could tell the girl was not communicating, that she was hurt, or angry or something of the sort. She could also tell that the boy was smitten with her. That young man? With Naomi Blue? Naomi Blue was almost forty. This boy was barely out of bloomers. But it didn't take a snoop to realize that the two had more going on than she had realized. No wonder she was late for work the other day. She was having an affair. With the boy. How interesting.

Ida Minsky came out to the front of the store. Naomi hastened to look busy.

"So, the boy was here."

Naomi turned to look at Ida. "The boy?"

"Yes, your boy."

"My boy?"

"Your boy. I'm not blind, you know. I may be an old woman, but I'm not blind. Or deaf."

"Oh, I'm sorry if I was talking too loud. I didn't..."

"No, no. I didn't mean that. I just meant that I heard your conversation."

"Oh."

"He seems like a sweet boy."

"Well, that's part of my problem, Mrs. Minsky, he seems like a boy. I am way too old for him. Way too old."

"Who cares about that sort of nonsense? If he doesn't care, why should you?"

"It's a lot of years."

"A lot. A lot. Who defines a lot? Why does it matter?"

Naomi wiped the table where Henry had been sitting. She pushed in the chair. "I don't know. I don't know why it matters. Maybe right now it doesn't matter to him. But it would. It could. It might in the future."

"Future? Darling, you have to stay in the present. The future? Don't you be worrying about the future. It will come soon enough."

"I don't know. I just don't know."

Ida Minsky looked at the girl. True, she was not really a girl at all. But she was young, really, so young. There were so many years ahead of her. She didn't know yet how fast they would go. She didn't know how quickly time would pass and she would be wondering why she hadn't lived.

Chapter Fifteen

Naomi Blue

LARGE FLAKES BEGAN TO FLOAT down gently at three o'clock. By four o'clock they were thick, and when Naomi looked directly up at the sky while she was walking, it was dizzying. Naomi Blue looked up and felt that swirl of space, the flakes coming down at her eyelids, into her open mouth. She was glad to be finally on her way home. Between Henry's visit to the bakery and Ida's inquisitiveness and lecturing comments, she wanted to go home and take a bath.

While she made a cup of tea, she let Beatrix out the back. The dog literally bounded and bounced around the yard, ecstatic—if one could put such a human emotion on a dog—in the snow. She jumped around, put her face in the snow, licked her nose, shook herself and then repeated the whole sequence. Naomi laughed. Dogs reminded her of how ridiculously complex her own life was. Just plant your face in the snow and all would be well, and be sure to shake off anything that bothered you. A dog's world of simplicity. She should try it.

She sank into the hot bathtub. Beatrix waited with her head on her paws outside the door. Naomi slid down so that her hair spread out in the water around her, flowing wildly about her shoulders. It felt good to relax. She shampooed her hair and slid back under to rinse.

She came back up and leaned back against the side of the tub. She sipped her tea. Henry. She liked him. She liked him more than she had admitted to herself. And the underlying fear of their ages had been partially alleviated when they had seen each other naked. Her fear wasn't simply about her physical age, but about the difference in their life stages. She was done with her thirties and the particular kind of optimism that came along with it. Optimism about starting a family, building a career and all the other things her friends in Maryland had been working towards. She realized that the end of her relationship with Will had put her out of sync with her peers. And now she was moving into some sort of undefined phase, one she hadn't expected, one that was more escaping than living. Moving to Copper Prairie shielded her from such reflections about where she was in her life, and that had been working pretty well until now. Henry, by being twenty-nine, reminded her of where she had been and was no longer. How could that work?

And in the midst of this unsettled feeling, there was Millie Bing's schoolgirl-like confession about her desire to date and "get" Henry. Millie and Henry were the same age and it made a whole lot more sense. What was their relationship anyway? Was anything going on there? It would be easier to just back away now.

Clean, muscles and tensions relaxed, Naomi got out of the bath. Without dressing, she crawled under the bedcovers. It was too early to go to bed for the night, but she was sleepy from the day and the bath. Just a bit of time with her eyes shut would be very, very nice.

Beatrix barked. Naomi Blue opened her eyes. She didn't remember falling asleep. She had the distinct sense of time having passed. Beatrix was standing beside the bed alert. Maybe she needed to be fed. Beatrix barked again.

She got up and put on a favorite threadbare pair of flannel pajamas. The house felt cold and oddly silent. Beatrix barked again and ran down the stairs with Naomi behind her. The dog went to the front door and stayed there. Naomi opened the door. Henry stood there with snow halfway up to his knees.

"Henry, what are you doing?"

"I've been standing at your door knocking. I thought maybe we could talk. You said we could talk later."

"Come in." Naomi looked outside past Henry. There was a lot of snow already. How long had she been sleeping? Henry was white with snow. He spread his wet clothes out in the front hall on the floor.

"Let me make us some tea," Naomi said.

"That sounds great. I'm really cold," Henry said gratefully. "Hey, are you in your pajamas?"

"Um, yeah. I wasn't expecting company."

"Sorry for coming by unannounced. I thought maybe you wouldn't talk to me if I called. You were sure giving me the cold shoulder at the bakery today. So I just stopped by."

"Well . . ."

"Do you see this snow? Man, I didn't realize that this was some major snowstorm. It's coming down so fast and hard. I haven't seen a storm like this since I was a kid."

"Said like a true Minnesotan. 'When I was a kid we would walk to school in two feet of snow,'" Naomi joked.

"No, really. This is some big snow."

Naomi relaxed into being with Henry again with his easygoing style, his unpretentious manner, and the fact that he could carry a conversation on his own. It wasn't hard to be with him. They picked out teas and waited for them to steep. The house was cold, and they sat facing each other, holding their mugs for warmth.

"Okay, Naomi, what's going on?" Henry's directness allowed little room for evasive answers. But where to start?

"Henry." That was a great place to start, Naomi chided herself silently. Keep going.

"Okay, Henry, so, well, there are two things going on. First, I had dinner the other night with a woman who wants you, lusts after you in fact, and made it sound like maybe you have something going on with her."

"What? Who? Who did you have dinner with?"

"Millie Bing."

"Millie Bing. Well, that's ridiculous. She's been after me since we ran into each other right after I moved back to town. But I'm not interested in her, and I've given her no reason to even think I am."

"She said you'd had drinks together a couple of times or something like that."

"I admit it—I go to Mikey's and the Ringworm alone. Maybe too often. Twice she sat down with me. Once was the first time I saw her after getting back to town. The second time she was totally smashed at Mikey's, and I ended up escorting her home. I'm sure she wouldn't have made it home any other way."

"Oh."

"I'm not interested—and have never been interested—in Millie Bing."

"Oh."

"I am, however, very interested in you. I wouldn't have stayed overnight if I wasn't. I don't do that sort of thing lightly."

"Oh."

"You're not saying much."

"I'm listening. And drinking my tea."

"Right. But you've got to understand that Millie Bing is just a girl I went to high school with. I didn't even remember her."

"Okay."

"What else? Is that it, Naomi?"

"Not really. I'm worried about this age thing, the difference between us, that maybe you want things I don't want, or will be disappointed in the fact that I'm in a different place, or whatever. I don't know. It's just this sense that we are too many years apart.

"Do I seem younger?"

"No."

"I think this is just something in your head. Can't you try just letting this unfold? It's too soon to put up roadblocks."

Naomi was quiet for a bit, sipping her tea, wondering if that's all she was doing, putting up roadblocks.

"I worry, Henry, that if this turned into anything, the differences will be more apparent. You would want kids, and I wouldn't, or something like that. I worry that I'll start to show physical signs of aging, and you'll be a decade or so behind me and be embarrassed to be with me or turned off or something like that. I worry that you'll want me until you conquer me and then you'll sleep with someone else while I'm at work. I worry—"

"Hey, Naomi. Hold on. That's not me. You're going to have to have a little faith in me. And let's see where we go."

Have a little faith in him. And have a little faith in myself too, she supposed. But it was much easier to let it all go and be her independent self. This stuff was just too complicated.

IDA MINSKY

IDA WAS WASHING DISHES. Rooster Robinson stood a few feet away, waiting with a dishtowel to dry. He wasn't handy in the kitchen, and this was about all he could do well. And even that was an exaggeration given the plate and one mug that had slipped from his hands crashing to the floor. Ida was glad for the help though. And for the company. Her hands deep in the sudsy water, she realized that she and Rooster were slipping into a comfortable domestic sort of pattern. Having their own stores meant they worked long hard hours and were apart most of the day. But when Roger knocked on her door and climbed slowly up the stairs with an armful of groceries, she felt cozy, a sense of comfort, and a sense of being connected. Maybe her time for love had come, if this was indeed love. They were companionable. They were friends. They seemed similar. Was it love? Maybe not. Maybe it was just comfortable. She wasn't sure she knew.

They spent time in her little apartment preparing supper, eating, cleaning up the meal, followed by tea. And then most nights, Roger would discreetly ask, "What about tonight, Ida?" and she would have the option of letting him stay or not. He never asked why she said no when she said no. If she felt uncomfortably full from dinner, as sometimes was the case, she would say no, too embarrassed to tell him why. He never argued the matter.

Sometimes she replied, "Yes, Roger, tonight would be a good night." With those words, Roger would pull down the shades overlooking the street, move one of the kitchen chairs over towards the window side of the bed, and begin to undress, draping his clothes over the chair. There was a matter of factness in his undressing. Ida had been appalled the first time she had watched this. Had she been expecting romance in his disrobing? She wasn't sure. But she did not undress in such a manner. It would be unbecoming. She would go to the bathroom where she now kept her nightgown and bathrobe, and begin her nighttime routine. Once undressed and then redressed in bedclothes, her face washed and her teeth brushed, her long hair unwoven from the braid and brushed out, nearly a full fifteen minutes from the time she went into the bathroom, Ida would emerge.

Tonight when she came out, Roger was already under the covers, but very much awake. She knew that any romance he showed would happen once the lights were out. For this, Ida was thankful.

She turned out the lights and took off her robe. She slid into bed and realigned her nightgown around her legs. Sometimes, he would be in his boxers. Tonight he was startlingly naked. He turned on his side to face her and came in closer. Ida wasn't exactly passive with him, but she usually waited to see what he was going to do first. He didn't talk much once they were in the bed, and this meant that if she had anything important to say it must have already been said. Ida waited. Roger moved his hands down to find the edge of the nightgown. Although Ida wasn't sure she heard right, she was pretty certain she heard him mutter "infernal nightgown" to himself. His hands found their way under anyway and she inched closer to him. It was pretty clear to Ida, with her rather limited experience with men, that Roger was far more experienced with women than she was with men. He seemed to know just how to touch her skin to make her shiver and want more, whether it was touching her neck, her arm, or elsewhere. He seemed to blend gentle with forceful, and was consistently loving. She loved nearly every minute of their lovemaking in the darkness. Well, in truth, sometimes it lasted too long when she was tired and his weight too heavy. But Ida figured that was all part of the deal. And while she liked sex, what she secretly liked even more was when they curled up together, his front against her back, and his arm laid possessively across her body. Once settled into this position for the night, Ida relaxed. And even when Roger fell hard into sleep within a few minutes and his arm felt too heavy on her, she stayed still enjoying the comfort of him against her. This made it all worthwhile . . . the sense of being protected and loved. And then Ida Minsky would sleep too.

Henry Alexander

Naomi Blue made them a light supper after their talk. Henry had already eaten supper but didn't want to mention it because Naomi was suddenly ravenously hungry. Her refrigerator didn't have much in it, but she pulled out a cutting board, lined up three different types of cheese sticking a knife into one, sliced up a couple of apples, and placed half a baguette on a plate as well. She poured two glasses of red wine from a bottle that unfortunately had been sitting on the counter too long. But he drank it anyway, commenting on its tartness.

Beatrix came and put her head on Naomi's lap. "Need to go outside?" she asked. The dog bounced back and headed towards the back door. Naomi switched on the outside light as she opened the door.

"Wow, look at this." Henry joined Naomi at the door. The snow was still falling, though a bit lighter than it had been. The tree branches were laden with snow, and there was nearly no wind at all. The dog was up to her haunches in snow. It was beautiful, the light glistening on the still falling snow.

"Henry, I don't think you're going anywhere tonight."

"Nowhere? Uh, what about upstairs?"

Naomi Blue smiled. He loved that smile. Beatrix came back inside and stood right beside them and shook off the snow. Naomi yelped.

"Let's go upstairs, Henry. She soaked me."

They went upstairs quietly, although eagerly. It seemed that they had moved past something this evening, past whatever was holding Naomi back from him. He had felt it lift.

He undressed her. It was a simple thing to do tonight since she had surprisingly little on. He hadn't realized when they had been talking that she was naked under her pajamas. It had simply never occurred to him. Henry had not lied to her tonight. He did not worry about their age difference. He saw it though. He saw it in the skin on her face, on her neck, in the softness in her stomach and breasts. But these were not turn-offs to him. They were just Naomi. She was utterly beautiful to him. Her fullness, her softness, her hips . . . he could not get enough of any part of her. And he did not feel younger than she was. They had both had their share of life, she just a little more. The compatibility between them was a rare gift, he thought. And it made him want her even more. Right from the start, when he met her at the bakery, he could not get enough of Naomi Blue. Even so, he took his time with her tonight, slowly and gently, so she would know how he felt.

They never heard the train.

Chapter Sixteen

Naomi Blue

"What day is it?" Henry asked her before she'd really woken up.

"I don't know."

"I do. It's Election Day. Tuesday. We've got to get up and vote."

"Henry, not yet. I'm not up yet."

"Yes you are. You're up. Come on. Let's get up."

"Not yet."

"It's my day. Let's vote. I need your vote."

Naomi turned on her side away from him. He was definitely a morning person. For a moment, she thought she'd gotten her way and been granted a few more minutes of sleep. But she was mistaken, if his hand coming around her waist was any sign of it.

"Okay, okay, I'm up!" Naomi groaned. His hand didn't move away. She rolled around so fast, he probably didn't realize what she was doing. He was underneath her.

"Oh really?" he asked.

"Really."

It was some time later that they finally got out of bed, Henry with a little less energy than he had started the morning with. But with no less enthusiasm for voting.

He looked out the front window. "Do you have a shovel?"

"Nope."

"What? No shovel? How can you not have a shovel? Maybe it's in that darn shed of yours."

"No, there's no shovel in there."

"How do you know? Did you get in?"

"Yeah, I found the key. All that was in there was a bunch of old stuff plus a rocking chair," she said. Naomi was not quite ready to share the rest of her discovery with Henry.

"Wow, a chair but no shovel. Well, do you have boots? Let's go out for breakfast and then go vote."

"How about we go vote and then you can walk me to Ida's. I have to work today. You can get some coffee and breakfast there."

They got dressed. Naomi's winter choices were minimal, but she layered as best she could and pulled on a pair of old winter boots she'd found in the back of the closet. They were probably Mr. Cooper's. With thick socks, they fit fine.

The morning was one of those perfect winter mornings. The sun had just risen, the snow had stopped, there was no wind, and the city plows had been through once, making a rough path for them to walk down. It was quiet. They trudged down to city hall to vote, walking in the middle of the road.

Naomi and Henry were the fourth and fifth people to vote so far. Henry seemed hopeful about his chances of being elected. The snow would affect voter turnout, but how that would affect his chances were unknown. The polls closed at eight o'clock in the evening. They would know the results soon enough.

Henry Alexander

After leaving Naomi at the bakery, Henry went on home. He was on edge about the election and just couldn't seem to relax. He sat down on his futon and turned on the television. And that's where he stayed for the next six hours. Like a boy home from school with the flu, he stayed there holding the remote, flipping from old movies to cartoons, to soap operas and the news. He didn't really care what he watched as long as it kept him from thinking about the election. The *African Queen* came on at two in the afternoon, and he watched that without even moving during the commercials until he finally dozed off.

The sound of a snowplow woke Henry up. He was disoriented from sleeping in the middle of the day. But he hadn't gotten too much sleep with Naomi Blue the night before, and he was making up for the loss. That kind of sleepless night was well worth the next day's exhaustion, he thought. Well worth it. He looked at the clock. The polls would close in a couple of hours already. Soon he would know if he was a city elder.

IDA MINSKY

THIS KIND OF SNOWFALL DIDN'T BODE well for the bakery's sales. And while the thought of shelves piled up with day-old bread did not appeal to Ida, the thought of not having enough goods to sell was even less appealing. So she baked her normal quantities. But as the day had gone on, she acknowledged that it had been a very slow day and there would be good deals for non-picky customers tomorrow.

The girl had yawned nearly the whole day through. She clearly wasn't getting enough sleep, or any sleep, if Ida was any judge of it. Naomi was quiet, and no matter how Ida tried to draw her out, she didn't talk about anything more than the snow. She was a private sort of person, Ida realized, but when the two of them were alone in the store with so few customers, she preferred it if she would be less withdrawn. Finally, Ida had enough.

"Naomi, go home."

Naomi turned at the abruptness of the comment and looked at Ida. "Go home?"

"Yah, you're yawning and moping around here all day. Go home and get some sleep. Just go."

Naomi unwound her apron slowly. "Are you mad at me, Mrs. Minsky?"

"I'm not angry, no. It's slow, too slow, and you're yawning so much it's enough to make me tired. So go home and get some sleep. I'm not mad."

"Okay."

"And take some of these rolls with you, or here, take this and this." Ida began to fill a large bag. "Take."

"Wow, thanks, that's a lot of stuff. Okay, enough," she said, trying to avoid the excessive quantity of bread and cakes Ida's generosity meant she would have to carry home. "That's great."

Naomi pulled on her boots and sweater and opened the door.

"Thanks, Mrs. Minsky."

"Shut the door! It's cold! Go home and sleep. And eat some cake."

With the girl gone, Ida made a fresh pot of coffee and sat down in the front window with a caramel roll. Eating alone made her feel guilty about adding calories to her already wide hips. But so good, it tasted so good. The view from the window wasn't quite so interesting with all this snow. The plows had come through and cleared the streets pretty well, leaving huge piles of snow at the curb. Soon, they'd come through and clear the sidewalks. Until then, it was going to be hard work to get to her front door. She realized that she should have had Naomi shovel a pathway for her before she left, but now it was too late. She contemplated getting the red shovel from the back closet and doing it herself, but that sounded like a lot of work. She stayed right where she was, drinking coffee.

"Ida!" The unmistakable sound of Rooster Robinson's voice came reverberating through the back of the store. During the day, he usually used the front door; at night, he came in through the back. "Where are you?"

Ida didn't get up. "I'm here having coffee."

Rooster Robinson came through to the front of the store, his large black pack boots leaving clods of snow as he traipsed through the bakery. Ida looked at the floor. He turned around looking at the floor to see what she was looking at. "I'm making a mess in here."

Ida snorted. "Ach, of course. Don't worry. It's one of those days. Look at the floor out here. Sloppy. Nobody wipes their feet on the mat anymore. Just come in like it's a garage. They don't think. They don't care. So don't worry. It's only snow."

"You need shoveling. Where's your shovel?"

Ida felt uncomfortable having Rooster shovel for her, not only because he was as old as she was, but also because she didn't like owing favors. But he had offered, he was a sturdy sort of man and there was no one else around. *Ah, well, let the man help. Men like to help. They like to do. Let him do it.*

"Back hall closet," she replied finally. Rooster Robinson left to shovel.

She felt guilty eating a sweet roll and guilty watching a man shovel her walk. She shook her head. *Ridiculous. Live it up. I deserve the sweet roll and the man deserves the chore.* She sat and watched him try to dig a path from the street up to the front door of the bakery.

NAOMI BLUE

THE PAPER SACK WAS NOT QUITE up to the demands of Ida's products. Before Naomi got halfway home, the bag had a small hole on the bottom. She carried the bag in front of her, awkwardly protecting the hole from expanding. Naomi wondered why she needed so much stuff anyway. Cold and her arms stiff, she finally reached her house. She dumped the assortment of breads and cakes out on her kitchen table and sat down. This is a lot of stuff. She opened a bag of thinly sliced caraway rye bread and took the very end piece, more crust than bread. It was good. She took the next slice, still really the heel. Before she even took off her boots, Naomi Blue had eaten half the loaf of rye. Not bad.

Henry Alexander

The call came at ten o'clock that night. The clerk, a woman who had worked at the town hall for forty-five years come June, had finally finished counting the ballots. She had counted them three times by hand, carefully tallying the votes of the candidates. There had not been many votes cast, most likely due to the snow, but this was a job that she liked to have absolute certainty about. She called the mayor first to inform him of the results. Then she called the candidates.

Henry listened as she congratulated him on his win. He listened as she recounted to him the number of votes he had received as well as the number of absentee ballots that had come in for him (two, to be precise, probably his parents in Arizona). He listened as she told him when he would be officially installed as a city elder. He listened to her chuckle in saying that he was the youngest city elder ever elected, by some thirty-eight years. He listened to all the details of the city clerk's phone call, but heard one thing. He had won.

Chapter Seventeen

Naomi Blue

The low rumble of the freight train woke Naomi Blue up well before she had intended to wake. She so rarely heard the train anymore, but she hadn't slept well. The night had been still and cold, stars vividly glittering across the northern sky due to the new moon. The temperature had dropped to an unusual low for November. The air in her bedroom seemed to have dropped to an unusual low as well, and she puffed out some air to see if she could see her breath. Comforted that she couldn't, she pulled her blanket over her head and listened to the train. The vases on her dresser vibrated. It was a long one this morning. Beatrix, realizing that Naomi had moved and might actually be awake, jumped up on the bed. She looked for Naomi's face, or any visible body part. Nothing was above the covers, so she curled into a tight ball of fur. Naomi closed her eyes and held still. The image of Henry pressed into her consciousness. She had managed to avoid too much serious thought about him and the direction their relationship was taking. She tried not to think too directly about him now. She was aware of an unsettled feeling though, and she knew it was distinctly related to him. And while she told herself to go back to sleep, it became clear that sooner or later she would need to figure out what was going on.

Since moving to Copper Prairie, Naomi Blue had managed to stay insulated from people. She hadn't realized how easy that would be. Despite the fact that she wanted to feel part of the community, she had slipped into the habit of keeping apart. Loneliness hadn't been a problem since working in the bakery and the window-modeling job kept her busy. Modeling kept her, well, out there. But quiet. Silent. No contact. Henry's persistence was changing things. He had drawn her into his world. And it had drawn him into her bed. Although he had many of the qualities she wanted in a man—funny, interesting, smart, warm, caring, generous—she wasn't sure she even wanted a man. Man? He was hardly that. Her age didn't seem to bother him at all, but she wondered if a relationship with such an age difference would last. She wondered if any relationship would last.

Staying awake under the covers on a cold morning was guaranteed to make her think. Naomi pushed aside her thoughts. No more pondering. She quickly got dressed, Beatrix close at her heels. The dog was excited simply by Naomi's rapid motions and clearly thought a well-deserved walk was the next activity. Pulling on the wool fisherman sweater, Naomi Blue opened the back door, pushed open the screen and let the dog fly past her.

Beatrix pawed the snow, uncovering a buried tennis ball. She crouched in the snow, licking the moisture from the ball. Naomi pulled the ball from Beatrix's slobbery mouth, tossed it across the yard, and waited while the dog bounded through the snow to retrieve it. She pulled the ever-increasingly soggy ball from the dog's mouth and threw it again and again. The bright day reflected off the snow, the sun warming her. When the snow finally melted through her soles to her feet, she realized it was time to go in. She turned to go back inside for some much needed coffee when she noticed footprints in the snow on the other side of the yard. She carefully stepped towards the trail made in the snow going from the train tracks around the shed to the shed door. Deep big footprints. They came from the back around to the front of the shed where the snow was tamped down fairly well. Naomi shivered. Someone had been poking around her yard while she slept. Someone had been there. The prints circled round the shed and seemed to return to the train tracks.

She looked around the yard. Quiet, listening. Beatrix was excited by her stillness and jumped around her, ball in mouth. The dog's noises imploring her to play made it seem less sinister. But she was unnerved. She stepped back into the kitchen, opened the birdcage and grabbed the shed key.

Naomi Blue went back over to the shed. Someone was interested in her shed. Now she had a sudden determination to understand the birdhouses, a need to understand who Lyle Cooper had been, or at least why he had hidden his work in the shed. She unlocked the padlock. The door seemed frozen shut, snow packing it in place. After some effort, the door finally opened enough for her to slip inside. The morning light through the half-opened door wasn't enough to see very well. Naomi stood there, hoping her eyes would adjust. Beatrix came near and warily sat just outside the door with the tennis ball firmly lodged in her mouth.

The bird houses, with their windows and doors, their perches and peaks, seemed to be faces, watching her from the walls. She stood quietly. Were they smiling or glaring at her? The light slanted in from the door, illuminating a small house, reminding her of the rocking chair with its multi-colored pieces of wood, shaped so beautifully into a peaked roof. She slid her fingers down the roof. She wiped the gritty dust off on her jeans. She tried to put a finger inside the narrow round birdhouse doorway. It didn't surprise her somehow to feel something in there. She angled a small piece of paper out with two fingers. She went outside to read it. Written in blocky print with a thick pencil, it was a random sort of sentence, maybe even a poem.

> "The pattern of our lives crossing like threads in a cloth, colors from the earth hues of clay and slate, an occasional streak of brilliance from the violet of the iris, simple threads, loosely woven in love."

Naomi felt the guilt of reading something private, something that wasn't hers to read. But it was hers, really, since this was her shed in her backyard. Yet the feeling of trespass lingered as she went back into the shed and slid the note back in its birdhouse home. She was the trespasser. She locked the shed. She glanced at the footprints. They were man-sized footprints, she was sure. She was not comforted by the stranger's visit.

IDA MINSKY

NOTHING COULD BE FURTHER FROM HER MIND today than Rooster Robinson. Nothing. It was a day to focus on the store and think about butter, flour, sugar, vanilla, eggs, and baking powder and the way these ingredients combined to bring joy. After getting her regular breads and cakes in the oven, she set her mind to a cookie she had never baked. It was a cookie she had eaten as a child. Without a recipe, she needed to rely on her memory to create it. Conjure it. Take sweet butter, fresh farm eggs, flour and sugar—and create dough the consistency of the perfect cookie. Thicker than sugar cookie dough, but softer than shortbread. In her mind, Ida could see the display of cookies behind glass in the bakery. She could see her own face in the reflection staring at the most exquisite cookies, each kind on its own tray, some dipped in chocolate, some with multi-colored sprinkles, some with raspberry jam between thin wafers, different shapes, shells and cut circles, pressed into the shapes of lovely creations. The choices. She remembered carrying home the box of cookies with its red-striped string that had been quickly tied in a bow. She remembered her mother admonishing her not to hold it by that string since that one morning when the string had slipped off and the cookies had tumbled from the box onto the sidewalk. Her mother had told her to leave them be, but she had put a few gritty cookies in her coat pocket anyway, and she had eaten them, despite her mother's warnings about horrible dirty diseases. It was too late for that, she had thought. She remembered the wonder and excitement when she slipped the string off the corners of the box and opened it to reveal those gorgeous cookies. All this went into Ida's need to create these cookies. The memory of cookies. The memory of the little girl she'd been. So on this cold morning, Ida began experimenting with differing quantities of butter, sugar, and eggs. She tried fine sugar, more eggs, a bit of sour cream. An extra egg. She tried more butter, less flour. Too thick. Too sticky. More this. More that. In front of four aluminum bowls were slips of cash register receipt paper with her notes for what went into each batch of dough.

Ida was so deeply focused on her cookies she didn't hear Naomi Blue open the front door. It wasn't until the girl was in the doorway to the back kitchen that Ida realized she was there. Ida jumped back in surprise.

"Ach. When did you get here?"

"Am I late, Mrs. Minsky? I don't think so. I'm—"

"I didn't hear you. Are the bells on the door?"

"Uh, yes, they are. They're working fine. What are you doing?"

Ida wiped her hands on her apron. What a silly question, was the girl making conversation? Blind?

"Cookies, Naomi. I'm baking cookies. Can't you see that?"

"Yes, I mean," the girl stammered. "I mean, today is Wednesday. What are you making cookies for? What kind of cookies?"

"A new recipe. Not a new recipe. But new for me. I'm making these special bakery cookies. The kind I ate as a girl. No recipe at all. I'm recreating them from memory. From taste."

Naomi leaned over the bowls, examining the differences between them. Ida was sure she wouldn't know one from the other.

"I'm trying to create a cookie for the Prairie Winter Bakeoff. I want to enter that contest. Win it. I haven't won a baking contest for some years. Probably could win a contest if I wanted to go to the state fair, but it's too far, too far to go. Too far to go in the heat. And too many people down there in the Cities, anyway."

Naomi nodded. She washed her hands and tied her apron.

"Well, I'm happy to be your taster."

"I'm sure you are, Naomi. Of that I am quite sure."

Ida spent much of the morning shaping the cookies, baking them at various temperatures. When they cooled, she dipped some into melted chocolate, some with sprinkles, some without, some with a thin layer of jam between them, laying them out on parchment paper to set. There were sprinkles all over the counter, and if Ida had looked closely in the mirror, she might have seen chocolate embedded in the creases of her face.

Naomi Blue

Eating cookies was not something Naomi Blue needed to be talked into. Ida Minsky set identical looking platters of cookies on the counter.

"We wait for Rooster Robinson," Ida said quietly. "He'll taste with us. Yes?"

"Sure," Naomi responded. Naomi was curious about Rooster's relationship with Ida, but knew it wasn't her place to ask about such a thing. After all, Ida was her boss, and someone who had managed to keep such great personal distance between them. Naomi knew little about Ida Minsky really. She wondered about her. She knew Ida was from Chicago and that her parents were immigrants, but even this bit of information was gleaned from snatches of conversation, not a real discussion of her life. Naomi wondered about that limp she had, and what had caused that. A bad hip, maybe. Or maybe it was just from being so wide. She didn't know. Most of the time, Naomi didn't notice the limp, it was so much a part of who Ida was. Ida hadn't mentioned a husband, so she didn't think she was widowed. Ida seemed interested in only one thing—the bakery. Until now, Naomi thought. She suspected that Rooster Robinson and Ida Minsky had a serious thing going on now. Ida was generally a little less abrupt with him than she was with most people. Besides, she called him Roger, and that must be a sign of something.

Rooster Robinson came in the front door. Naomi knew he sometimes showed up at the back door, even sometimes while she was up front wiping down counters. She would hear Ida's hushed tones telling him to wipe his feet and then shortly after, she'd hear him leave again. But when he was coming to eat something, he came through the front door like any other customer.

"Hello, Mr. Robinson," Naomi greeted him.

"Ah, yes, hello, Miss Naomi." He dragged his feet back and forth along the gray carpet at the door. He nodded deeply at Ida and took an audible intake of air through his nose.

"Smells magnificent in here!"

Ida Minsky gestured him to the counter where the four plates of cookies waited.

"This is a taste test, Mr. Robinson. Take one cookie from each plate and tell me what you think."

"Only one?"

"Ach, yes, only one. For now. And I want to know which cookie you like the best. But don't tell me right away. Yes? Keep it to yourself. You too, Naomi."

Naomi and Rooster began with the first plate and worked their way to the last. Naomi was embarrassed to admit that she didn't notice a difference amongst any of the cookies. They were all good. She wondered if she could go for a second round.

"Well?" Ida asked, her hands on her wide hips. "What do you think, Naomi?"

"I think, um, I like them all. They were all good, really, Mrs. Minsky. I guess that's no help."

Ida Minsky raised her eyebrows and turned towards Rooster. Naomi was pretty sure her own ignorance and lack of palate had put an added burden on Rooster, a man whose taste buds must surely be less sensitive than her own. But perhaps he had more tact, she wondered.

"Let me see," he began. "May I have more before I speak?"

"Yes," Ida said slowly.

"May I have a glass of milk to wash the cookies down? You know, cleanse my palate?"

"Yes," Ida said, going to the rack of dishes for a glass.

Roger ate one more cookie from each plate. Between each cookie, he looked thoughtful, took a swig of milk, carefully swallowed, and went to the next plate. There was much drama in his movements. Naomi began to smile.

"Well?" Ida was getting impatient.

"Just a moment, Ida." Roger finished the glass of milk, wiped his mouth on his sleeve and let out a rather rude but contented belch.

"Excuse me," he apologized half-heartedly. "The cookies, Mrs. Minsky. The cookies are all good."

"You ate a dozen cookies and that's all you have to say?" Ida was clearly exasperated.

"I especially like the ones with raspberry preserves and chocolate. Very tasty."

"That's it?"

"Of the four plates, I like this one, the third one. Yah, those cookies are slightly lighter, less dense, good. Very good, my Ida."

Ida blushed and looked at the plate. "Okay then. Thank you, Roger. Naomi, you have a flat mouth. No good for taste testing."

"I did like them all, really. What's a flat mouth?"

"You like anything with sugar equally. Flat."

Naomi felt dismissed somehow, that she had failed a test, and a bit uncomfortable with the three of them standing around the plates of cookies. Thankfully, the door opened once again and she was able to wait on some customers.

Henry Alexander

Henry was ready to celebrate. But first, he called his parents to let them know.

"Mom?" he said when the call was answered.

"Henry, what's wrong? Why are you calling this early?"

Henry glanced at the clock and realized that he had neglected to take into account the time difference with Arizona. But even so, he didn't think it was too early to call. Maybe his parents had begun to sleep late in the morning, too hot out there to be up anyway.

"Um, sorry Mom. I was just calling to tell you that I won the election. I'm a city elder."

The silence that followed was brief, but unmistakable.

"Congratulations, Henry."

"Thanks. I can't believe it."

"Wait a minute, your father wants to talk to you," she said, clearly fumbling with the phone as she passed it to his father. Henry could so clearly picture the phone beside his mother's side of the bed, on the nightstand with her glasses and the tall glass of water she insisted had to be beside her at night. And he could see the phone being passed over to his father, who had turned away hoping for more time asleep, but who heard it was his wayward son on the phone and was suddenly eager to get a few words of advice across the miles.

"Henry."

"Yes, Dad?"

"I heard you won. Congratulations. But what about a job? A real job? Have you made any headway on that? Had any interviews?"

"Uh, not yet."

"Son, it's time for you to get serious. Find yourself a job. We can't continue to supplement your living expenses."

"Yeah, I know. I'm working on it."

"Good, very good. Okay, here's your mother." More fumbling with the phone.

"We love you, Hank."

"Love you too, Mom." He hung the phone up slowly. This was why he didn't call them too often. These phone calls left him feeling inadequate, with the clear impression that he didn't live up to their expectations, or at least, his father's expectations. Winning the election for city elder didn't seem to matter too much to him. Henry wondered if he was expecting too much of his father.

He sat back on his futon. He couldn't deny the fact that he wasn't taking the path his parents thought he ought to take or expected him to have taken. They had been pleased to see him go to school in Minneapolis, rather than staying home and attending the community college. But leaving the Twin Cities and returning to Copper Prairie wasn't what his parents thought was "in his best interest." But home was Copper Prairie, not Minneapolis. And he had had his fill of the people there—the hippie wannabes in their long skirts, hemp necklaces, and peace sign t-shirts; the college kids who roamed the streets in their identical North Face fleece jackets and flip flops; the middle-aged crowd in their pricey high-tech "breathable" winter clothes; and all the women. All the women with their piercings and tattoos. Sometimes you didn't even see them until you were in bed with them, and then it was a naked show and tell of sorrow and remembrance as they explained the story behind each one. It was a relief to move north and just live. Maybe it wasn't as different in Copper Prairie as he liked to believe it was. But the bars seemed more a place to be than a place to be seen at. And people talked more about the high school football team or the Fourth of July "On the Range Baseball Tournament" than whether the Twins won or lost. Maybe Henry had moved back to his memory of Copper Prairie, rather than the reality of it. But whatever it was, it was his home. And he was a city elder.

Chapter Eighteen

Naomi Blue

As usual, Naomi let Beatrix out as soon as she got home from the bakery. The dog looked delighted when Naomi stepped outside with her. She scampered around the yard looking for a ball, hoping there would be a game of fetch or tug of war. She busied herself finding the ball in the snow. Naomi went over to the shed. Early snows in Minnesota sometimes stuck around for the rest of the winter, but this one came before the ground was frozen. The sun was strong enough to melt much of the snow during the day, dissolving the stranger's boot prints into oblivion. Once again, Naomi unlocked the shed. Stepping inside, she breathed in deeply. Impulsively, she stuck a finger into the two-story birdhouse on the right side of the shed, fishing around. Nothing. What was she thinking? That all the houses had notes in them? Feeling foolish, Naomi began to stick her fingers in birdhouse after birdhouse, looking for notes. She found another one in a small ordinary looking house down near the ground. She carefully unfolded the paper, which seemed to be older, more brittle than the last one.

> "Meet me Tuesday. The moon's glow is a shadow of a dream, frost upon the ground and winter's light in my eyes. I think of days yet to dawn and moments yet to see your eyes and touch your cheek. Meet me here."

Naomi Blue refolded the note and put it back where she'd found it. She locked the shed, tossed the tennis ball four times, and then went back inside to find something to eat for supper, the dog close behind. The birdhouses and the notes didn't make a lot of sense to her. She was intrigued though, and it moved her, as if someone had been writing notes to her. Love notes hidden in birdhouses had a romantic feel to it, despite the mystery behind them.

With the sun setting early, the days had a certain quiet to them. The house echoed and was cold, even though she'd raised the thermostat. It didn't seem to make much difference with the old drafty windows. There were no shades on them and turning lights on at night made her feel exposed, even though no one lived close enough to peer in on her. She felt most comfortable upstairs in her bedroom. She made herself some toast, put a chunk of butter on each slice, heated up the cold morning coffee and headed upstairs. What she owned—what material things were left of her life—inhabited this bedroom, and really, it didn't amount to much.

Sitting cross-legged on the bed, she used her pinky to spread the now-melting butter around the toast. Eating in bed wasn't something she was proud of. She realized the inevitability of crumbs in the bed. But she no longer answered to anyone, and her sense of what was proper and right was fading along with the person she once was. Besides, this was the warmest place in the house. Who cared and who would know. Beatrix curled into a ball on the area rug, and in moments, was gently snoring.

Of course by isolating herself upstairs on this cold night, Naomi Blue was unaware of anything untoward happening outside. Nor was Beatrix, too fast asleep in the upstairs bedroom to be much use as a watchdog. So it was that someone explored the old shed once again without Naomi Blue even sitting up to listen to the noise in the wind. But after all, this was a woman who had learned to ignore freight trains rumbling through the night.

Henry Alexander

With the election results now public and Henry being hailed in the *Copper Press* as the youngest city elder in the town's history, his need for Naomi Blue was peaking again. She had called to congratulate him on his win, and had said she was too busy to see him. He felt put off. Henry was beyond reason with wanting her. He wondered if her distance on the phone was a message, wondered whether she was truly less interested in him, and wondered if she was interested in someone else. He was simply making himself crazy. What he was sure about was that he had to see her. While he didn't want to appear overly pushy, he seemed to have less control over his feelings than he liked. He called her.

The phone rang. After fourteen rings, he hung up. Maybe she was out. Maybe she was at the Ringworm. It was worth a try.

The Ringworm's window was the dark color of amber ale. But looking in, he could still see it was crowded and was hopeful to find Naomi. His eyes adjusted slowly as he stepped in the door.

"Ah, well lookie here. Look who has graced our humble abode."

It was Millie, and, no surprise, she had been there some time already.

"This isn't your abode, Millie," Henry replied, looking around the bar for Naomi.

"Well, that it isn't. That it isn't," she repeated.

He looked at Millie who was pressing ever closer to him.

"You okay?" he asked.

"I'm juss fine, Elder Hank. But finer now that you came in."

"Right . . ." Henry was wary of Millie, the smell of alcohol bridging the distance between them. He looked around for Naomi.

"Are you meeting someone here, Hank?" Millie persisted.

"Just looking for a friend," he said distractedly looking around the bar. Naomi did not seem to be here.

"A friend? Who?"

"Uh, Naomi Blue."

"I know Naomi Blue," Millie said. "She's that girl who models at the Carriage General. I know her."

"Oh, yeah," Henry replied, focusing now on Millie, the tone in her voice shifting, making him feel warned somehow.

"Come on, sit with me. Have a beer. I'm sitting at the bar all by my lonesome. I need some company. Come on, elder man."

Henry wasn't eager to sit with her and drink. His mind was on finding Naomi. But Millie had his arm and was pulling him determinedly towards two empty stools. He figured one beer wouldn't hurt as he swung himself around on the stool.

"So, how've you been, Hank? I haven't seen you around too much. What've you been up to? Why are you looking for Naomi Blue?"

It was only then, after wiping the first taste of the beer's foam off his upper lip, that he remembered Naomi's jealousy about Millie, about her saying that Millie was interested in him, and his avowal that he was not interested in Millie. And he was not. But the woman was so open to him, leaning on her elbow, laying her upper body on the edge of the bar, towards him, her shirt open, and she was so, well, so available. They drank in silence. He knew it was dangerous sitting here with Millie. Millie lifted her mug up. He met it with his. She looked at him, eagerly, as if to draw him in. He wanted to look away, to not be interested, and to not give her anything. But his wanting, that powerful feeling he had for Naomi, but still so basic a need, combined with the second beer the bartender had quickly served and he was now enjoying, made Henry lose rational thought. He felt like reaching over to touch her, just inside her blouse, she was so eager. He leaned over to her, and she was already leaning into him to meet the kiss. It wasn't a long kiss because as quickly as he tasted her, he changed his mind. He backed off abruptly.

Millie's mouth was frozen mid-kiss and her eyes half shut. "What?" she said, more as a statement than a question. "What's wrong?"

"I'm sorry. It's not you. I'm not sure why I did that. I, uh, I'm sorry about that." He quickly drank some beer. Millie turned away from him, for which he was grateful. She might be mad, but it was a better option that going down that path with her.

"You're dating Naomi Blue?" she asked without affect.

The question surprised him. "Naomi Blue? Uh, yeah, actually, we are kinda seeing each other."

Her silence didn't surprise him. "I'm sorry, Millie, I didn't really mean to kiss you. I mean, it just happened and I'm sorry. You look great, really nice, and well . . ." He heard how ridiculous he sounded. But he wanted to make amends so he could get out of there.

Millie didn't look back at him again. She continued to be involved with her beer and began a conversation with the bartender. She ignored him entirely. He touched her arm lightly and said good-bye. Maybe Naomi was over at Mikey's.

That was unpleasant, Henry thought as he stepped outside, the cold air washing away the lousy feeling he had. Why had he done that? He felt like a jerk. He put a piece of gum in his mouth.

He met up with the heavy scent of too many people too close together inside Mikey's. The band was a local bunch of guys he vaguely remembered from high school. A considerable number of the kids he graduated with hadn't left Copper Prairie after graduation, finding themselves jobs on the range or in town, and in some ways, continuing their high school lives as they neared thirty. The music was loud, an angry sort of rock, and it made him feel edgier than he already felt. If Naomi wasn't there, he wasn't going to linger. He left quickly and headed home.

Chapter Nineteen

Naomi Blue

People might think it was easy to stand in a window wearing nice clothes and looking blank, but it wasn't really. It took an internal calmness to pose without fidgeting. And that was something Naomi did not naturally possess. To get to that place was a progression. First, Naomi entered the Carriage General. Some days Sebastian Skinner remembered her, and other days, he greeted her like a customer he hadn't met before. Some days he remembered her name was Naomi and other days he knew her name but couldn't recall she worked there. He was rather unpredictable. Sebastian Skinner laughed about his lack of recognition, pretending he was "just joshing" or otherwise teasing her. But once it was clear that it was Naomi Blue, his window model, Sebastian Skinner would become uncharacteristically spirited, picking out clothes for her outfit with a definitiveness that made it seem he had planned it all out ahead of time. He loved to dress her up.

The next step in her self-calming routine occurred when she stepped out of the dressing room wearing the clothes. She was transformed. Even with her lack of experience with anything related to fashion, Naomi knew she was hardly being dressed in the height of fashion. Sebastian Skinner's clothes were stale, she thought, though eventually the outfits might be back in style. He dressed her in prairie skirts, plaid western-style blouses with pearl snaps, denim skirts six inches above the knee, sweater sets, and an occasional skinny-strapped cocktail dress (despite the fact that she never saw a dress like that on the women's clothing racks in the store). Sebastian put her in heels, a challenge both in finding her size 10 in stock and in her ability to stand straight without toppling over. But this completed Naomi's shift from Bakery Naomi to Model Naomi. And as she stepped up into the window, she found her place on the far side of the ledge and took her position using a stool particularly when dressed in the spikiest of heels. Then she looked out at the bank, falling into a meditative state of relaxation.

Sebastian Skinner

Sebastian watched her from his chair behind the register where he pretended to read the *Copper Press*. He could only see her profile from this angle, but it let him forget time. So much time had gone by. The town had changed so much. It retained much of its traditions and what outsiders called "quaintness," but he knew it was changing despite this. Some of the other towns around had been forced to rely on tourism to stay alive. Some of those towns now had stores solely devoted to coffee, with computers lined up along the walls. What did those people even do on the darn things? Why not talk over a cup of coffee? Some towns had capitulated carelessly into change. Just a morning's drive north was a village whose chamber of commerce had discussed ways to lure the Twin City affluent to visit, spend some money—and had even built a hotel and conference center to entice them. Decorated in roughly hewn timber, wolves and moose, Sebastian Skinner felt they had sold out to profit. He didn't want Copper Prairie to become one of those towns. Keep those rich city folks down in the Cities. No need for them up here. He looked at the girl in the window. Her profile was strong. Wanda. Wanda was such a girl. Curvy. From the day this Naomi girl walked in the door, he saw Wanda. Wanda had those same curves, extra in the top and those hips, those hips he couldn't get out of his mind. And, brother, did she ever know it. Wanda loved to shop. At least she'd loved to shop at his store. That woman sure knew how to flirt. She knew precisely how strong a hold she had on him with all her teasing. And then there was Lyle, his best friend. It wasn't right to be smitten with his best friend's girl. It just wasn't right. But there was nothing to be done about it back in high school. Just pretend it wasn't so. But she knew. Changing into outfit after outfit behind the curtained dressing room, laughing as she came out in a pencil skirt and crisp white blouse, turning around in front of the mirror, admiring, knowing that he was watching. It was too much sometimes. Too much. She knew he watched her. She flaunted her curves around that store, as no other girl had ever flaunted.

Naomi Blue came down from the window, stepping carefully in the heels. Sebastian Skinner was carefully writing something on a small piece of paper. He had forgotten she was in the window. He was deep in thought about what he was writing. He glanced up at her. He looked at Naomi in an odd way. She looked away, uncomfortable. *That's not Wanda*, Sebastian thought. It wasn't Wanda. He forced himself to be in the present. He took the note and quickly folded it and shoved it way down in his trouser pocket.

"Pick whatever you want today, honey. You worked hard."

Clearly Naomi loved the moments when Sebastian Skinner told her what she could have in exchange for modeling. Sometimes, he told her what genre to choose from—shoes, winter clothes, purses. And then, some days like today, it was free choice. She went up the staircase to the home goods department.

Sebastian Skinner felt pangs of emptiness when Naomi Blue left the store. It wasn't an unusual feeling for him, but it seemed strangely associated with this girl. It was a loneliness rooted in time. He suffered from knowing that there were more days behind him than in front of him—this was his unassailable truth. Before Lyle passed away, they had talked briefly about it one night around a rickety card table playing casino, a game they shared a love of. He'd asked Lyle if he ever thought about that, about how they were truly senior citizens now, not just seniors, and not just citizens. Lyle had laughed as he'd shuffled the cards. So get me a cigar, he'd said. It can't hurt me now, can it? They'd both laughed, though it wasn't really funny, Sebastian thought. This truth. He acknowledged the passing of time, and yet couldn't quite accept it.

And now he missed Wanda. Wanda—the girl who he had quietly loved for so many years. In the beginning, Wanda knew and teased him, loving his attentiveness, which was even more attentiveness than Lyle gave her. And then finally, when Lyle was in the service, Sebastian had been there for her. He took her to dances and out for sodas. He drove her if she needed driving. He held her hand during movies. He was her constant and reliable companion. They never spoke about the times they found themselves alone, allowing their lovemaking to exist in silence. In privacy, his gentleness combined with her fierceness. He did not understand it. But there it was, this physical relationship, this basic bond, and it did not need words. Sebastian had never spoken of his feelings to Wanda, could not articulate them if he had even thought that appropriate. He knew he had no true claim on her. Wanda never spoke of her feelings towards him either. Their complicit silence protected them from the reality of the situation. She was Lyle's, although she gave herself to Sebastian regularly. Sebastian was, however, profoundly in love.

Lyle returned from the service and Wanda returned to Lyle. Still, no words were said. It was as if the intervening years had not happened. Sebastian honored his friend's return by taking Lyle, Wanda, and the rest of their friends out for a night on the town.

It was that very night that Sebastian found himself scribbling a note to Wanda and pressing it into her palm when Lyle had been in the restroom. She hardly acknowledged it, and never spoke of it, but his brief "Love." had been received. As for his violation of his friendship with Lyle, Sebastian Skinner was not concerned. It made him uneasy, but he had taken care of Wanda, and she mattered above any loyalty he might have felt towards Lyle.

Wanda. Sebastian had mistakenly thought that when Lyle passed away, it would be his time. Perhaps without ever thinking these exact thoughts, he had assumed it for a long time. He had waited all these years for her. But she had not spoken to him at the funeral. He tried to be respectful, to give her space, not to be aggressive. She did not seem to see him; he could not catch her eye. He watched her carefully for any sign. Her thinned gray hair pulled tightly into a small twisted bun. Her hands curved around a coffee mug, hands he'd known so long though they had changed over the years, the now spotted skin thin over the narrow bones in her fingers. But he had waited so long. In her house after the funeral, after walking down the road to have refreshments, his heart ached so badly he thought he might be having a heart attack. He'd rubbed his chest through the scratchy starched shirt under his only black suit, hoping to ease the pain. But she did not speak to him. A simple card had arrived two weeks after the funeral thanking him for his flowers and signed, "Best wishes, Wanda." Best wishes. Life was too quiet now. She had slipped away.

The model brought time back. Sebastian knew the girl wasn't Wanda. But sometimes, he felt Wanda was there. It was a slipping in his mind, a sense of reality fused with a sense of mistiness, confusion. Like a daydream he had held onto for so long. The girl brought him back in time. Sometimes he started to call her Wanda, though he sensed that wasn't the right name. Sometimes he wasn't sure what he had called her but since she always responded, perhaps he got it right. It was indeed fuzzy.

Naomi Blue

"I stand beneath the oaks finding peace in the dusk while clouds like dreams pass above me in the sky and my heart whispers its sweetness in the night, though you do not hear me. Despite your love, I stayed. With your love, I stayed."

Naomi read the note again. She had pulled it out of one of the birdhouses, seeing the corner of the paper sticking up just slightly when she opened the door that afternoon. It was in the birdhouse that looked like it had been made from an old picket fence. She didn't understand the note. She didn't understand the birdhouse shed at all. Who wrote the notes, she wondered, and why would he have put them in the birdhouses? Why would Lyle have hidden notes to his wife?

Naomi Blue took the dog for a late afternoon walk. Beatrix wasn't getting enough exercise as usual and that generally meant she wasn't either.

Henry Alexander

The sky had turned a dusky blue as it sometimes does in northern Minnesota, particularly before a mild day. As Naomi walked up the John Moore Road towards the cemetery, Henry was walking towards her house, hoping to spend some time with her. There had been a distance between them. He could not always read Naomi Blue and found the best way to understand her was to see her face, not talk on the phone. Whatever walls she brought up repeatedly between them were easier to break down in person.

He usually found that just showing up was a better way to get to see her than trying to arrange something. Although his mother taught him that dropping by unannounced was bad manners, with Naomi Blue it was the best way not to be rejected. Henry didn't understand her moods and her attempts to keep a distance. Maybe she was scared of relationships or maybe it was just something about him. But he was positive she was interested. When they were together, he was certain of her feelings. It was between those times that he lost track of the relationship and she seemed indifferent. Maybe it was time to talk about it.

Sebastian Skinner

As Henry was making his way down the road to Naomi Blue's house, Sebastian Skinner was closing the store a little earlier than the posted five o'clock time, putting on his black Sorel snow boots with the doubly thick wool felt liners, his black wool skull cap, and the tan canvas jacket lined with red and black buffalo plaid flannel. He noticed that the jacket could use a washing, traces of blood from his last grouse hunting adventure spattered along the pocket. He crossed through town to the railroad tracks. The track bed was slightly raised, and he had some difficulty getting his now clumsy legs up to the rails. This used to be so simple. How many years had he done this? But now it winded him. He felt old. As he stood finally on the tracks, right in the center, he looked north and then south. The only sound was the wind creaking the branches, finally barren of leaves. It wasn't easy walking on railroad tracks. It never was, he recalled. His stride was too long for two ties, so sometimes he stepped on the wooden ties and other times on the large pieces of crushed rock that filled the gaps between. Sebastian slowly made his way down the tracks. As a boy, he'd walked these tracks as a shortcut home from school. He'd kissed his first girl on these tracks, so moved he was by the possibility offered in the distance he could see in the never-ending length of rail. And of course, the privacy of the location had emboldened him. For years, he'd walked these tracks to Wanda Cooper's house, even while she and Lyle slept upstairs, even while no one knew he was there, so possessed by his love for the woman. He most often walked to the house at night, when it was safest. But there were times he was even there in the daylight, hiding behind the backyard garden shed. He wore his hunting camouflage sometimes, hoping to blend in with the tall prairie grasses. That worked until the year Wanda took up gardening with a vengeance, ordering bulbs and perennials from a catalog with tulips on the cover, the same one he got and stuffed in his boots for extra warmth in the winter. She put in those colorful flowerbeds along the back in front of the train tracks. He had little hope of blending in.

After so many years of walking the tracks, Sebastian hardly thought anything odd about it. He needed to see her. He wanted contact with Wanda, even if it were simply a glimpse of her through the trees. In the beginning, he was certain Wanda didn't know he was there. But as the years passed, she did know, or at least, she must have known. He saw her at the window one twilight evening, her face framed by lace curtains. He saw her look directly at him, before she lowered the shade, which she did only occasionally. Most times, the shade would be left up, and he watched, hoping to see her unbutton her blouse. No, it wasn't to see her undress, that was not why he watched. He needed to see Wanda's eyes. He had only seen her unbutton her blouse one time, and he had been ashamed, ashamed that he watched and ashamed at his arousal. Sebastian needed to have her in his life. It was simple. He would watch her at the kitchen window, head lowered over the sink, perhaps glancing outside, her dark bob swinging back as she looked up, soapy water on her hands, not wanting to brush back her hair with her wet hands.

It was on one such occasion that Sebastian noticed Wanda coming out the back door. Sebastian had skulked deeper into the brush. How could he ever have explained what he was doing back there? He watched carefully, as silently as if he were hunting grouse or the wild turkey that sometimes flocked across the fields west of town. He watched as Wanda went to the little crab tree, pulled gently down on the branch holding the birdhouse and removed something—and then opened the lock on the shed and went inside. Terrified of discovery, Sebastian took that opportunity to quietly escape back north on the tracks.

And so he walked this late fall day down the tracks back to Wanda's house. The tracks ran so close to the house, he could be practically in the backyard. He stood there watching, his hands thrust into his pockets. He felt the folded note that he'd written earlier for Wanda. Years of notes he pressed into her hand. Many notes he'd left for her in places she alone would find. Sebastian drifted in time, his memory blending with the present in a misty sort of way. Wanda's move to Florida was something he knew, a fact of sorts. And yet, at the moment, it was lost. He didn't remember that her grown children had packed up boxes and moved her themselves in an orange truck to an apartment in a senior community near the inland waterway. All those things were somewhere in his mind. But right now, chilled by the fall air, he simply knew that this was Wanda's house and that he loved her. Reality became a blend of past and present. An outsider might have said that Sebastian Skinner was confused. He didn't feel confused. It was merely the falling of walls between memory and reality. He waited.

Henry Alexander

Henry had finally gotten to Naomi Blue's house and knocked on the front door. No answer and no barking dog. He walked around towards the back. "Naomi?"

No dog and no Naomi. But he thought he saw a figure on the tracks. He stepped further into the yard and was certain that there was a guy in a black beanie, walking slowly, nearly stumbling, on the tracks. Must be a bum, Henry thought. Creepy. The tracks were so close to her house, maybe this happened more often than he realized. Must be hoping to hop on a train or something. Henry wanted to see him more clearly, feeling a sense of protectiveness about Naomi and pushed through the dense brush to get to the tracks. It was getting colder. There was the man, his shoulders hunched up, walking away in the dusk.

As Henry turned to go back towards the house, he noticed his socks and pants were covered in cockleburs, prickly and stuck deep enough into the fabric to be noticeable. He stood there pulling them off, half amused and half irritated to be doing this, a city elder of all people, walking haphazardly into the burs.

Finally free of most of the cockleburs, Henry started to leave the yard. But it had gotten dark and he noticed a light turn on in the house. He saw Naomi Blue at the kitchen window. She looked out. Could she see him? Now he'd be the peeping tom city elder. How would that look? He stood still. No, she didn't see him. She turned her back on the window, and Henry took that opportunity to slip out of sight and back up the road to his apartment on Oak Street.

Chapter Twenty

Ida Minsky

Ida Minsky was not excited by change. She liked routine whether it was the schedule she kept for baking or the time she woke up in the morning. For so many years life had been predictable. To Ida, this wasn't boring. It was just life's flow, day to day and year to year. She didn't dream about a cruise or retirement, like some people her age. She never even considered retirement. The bakery was her life. It was a good life. Hiring Naomi Blue had been a big decision, unnerving even, and a change in how she ran the bakery, but the girl was working out fine. She was a bit odd, but reliable, pleasant to be around, and careful not to ask for days off to work her second job over at the Carriage General. Ida had hired her before Sebastian had, and she felt possessive and not willing to share her with him, particularly not for modeling of all things. Not only did Naomi treat customers well but her willingness to take on all the front-end responsibilities allowed Ida to focus on her baking. And on Roger.

Roger Robinson had utterly changed her routine. It was more than changing her toiletry habits. Roger was who she thought about during the day. It was what she did in the evening. No longer did Ida sit at the window, watching the town grow dark. No longer did she have the entire double bed to sleep in. No longer did she cook for one. Now Rooster was also residing in her mind. She would watch the wind blow the snow horizontally and wonder how business was for him. She wondered if he saw what she saw from his store window. She wondered if he'd stay the night. She wondered if he loved her. Or if love mattered anyway. Some days she believed it was his sheer masculine physical presence that she most loved, his body hot in sleep on the mattress beside her. It was not lovemaking that she longed for but his arm over her waist while he was deep in sleep. Maybe she even liked that sense of ownership she associated with that heavy arm. She rarely lifted it off even when it kept her awake. She liked the sheer weight of it. Roger provided companionship. Friendship. He appreciated her bakery creations.

They did not talk too much over supper. At mealtimes, he was quiet, focused on the food and growling appreciative words about her cooking, though she knew she was an ordinary cook. He loved her hot dishes and devoured them, particularly the ones made with canned soup. There he was, rumpled and content across from her at the table.

And though he spent more nights with her than not, there were moments after he left her, the door closing firmly and the lock turned, that she felt the silence of his absence.

Was that love? Friendship? Security? Or was it something else entirely? Ida was not sure she knew, but it didn't matter. As long as life readjusted to this new "predictable," she would be okay.

Henry Alexander

Henry's election as city elder did not seem to matter to the people that he wanted it to matter to. His parents were barely amused by his election and continued to harp on him about his future. They eventually conceded that perhaps this was a steppingstone to something bigger, but he knew they were disappointed in him. Naomi Blue remained distant and he was trying to restrain himself from pushing her too hard. He hoped if he gave her space, perhaps she would come looking for him. Clearly his election as city elder didn't matter much to her either.

His first couple of visits to the Ringworm after winning the election brought him a couple of free beers, but that didn't last. At Mikey's, a round of applause went up that first night, but after that, he was just the guy who he had been before—someone who hung out most evenings with the rest of them, hoping for a good band or a competitive game of darts. But Henry was proud of winning the election and becoming the youngest elder ever. He was eager to be sworn in and begin that work. The position came with a small stipend based on the number of meetings per year and a second stipend for fulfilling his public duties by attending community functions, including the high school football games. He was sure he'd be attending everything possible.

However, Naomi Blue's distance was clearly having an impact on Henry. He was aware of the obsessive behavior that surrounded his routine. He walked at least once a day past the Carriage General hoping to see her in the window. Her appearances there seemed random and if he didn't go by multiple times in a day, he might miss her. If she were modeling, he would stop across the street and lean back against the side of the bank's brick wall and watch. He had discovered that she almost seemed to be looking at him when he stood by the bank. There was a physical excitement to this obsession, though he was certain no one had noticed. He would stand there watching Naomi as long as she held the pose. Her outfits varied in style although Henry didn't think any of it particularly stylish. Maybe it was stylish in another time, but she never quite looked like the girls he had dated. She looked a bit like a woman from the forties in those tight mid-calf skirts, white blouses, and high heels. She hardly looked like herself. He loved it. The Naomi Blue of his fantasies.

When she wasn't modeling, he would go around the block and end up at Ida's Bakery. From outside the bakery he could see her in that pink t-shirt and apron. He would feel a distinct nervousness in his stomach accompanied by the compelling need to be closer to her. His whole body would tense up as he pulled open the door.

Today Naomi was working at the bakery. He hesitated before going in. He tried to achieve a sense of self-control. *Just go in*, he told himself. *See her.*

He went into the bakery. "Hi," Henry said quickly, even before the bells on the door stopped their announcement. Naomi Blue looked up from where she was opening a roll of quarters into the register drawer.

"Hi, Henry. Can I get you something?"

Henry walked up to the counter. He looked at her hands working the quarters, watched her unroll the paper and dump the money in. She tossed the wrapper and looked at him.

"What?" she asked. "What?"

"I, uh, hey, Naomi. Let's hang out later, okay? I would love to see you."

Naomi Blue wiped her hands on her apron nervously.

"Come on, Naomi. It's good. This is good."

"Okay. Why don't you come over for dinner?" she asked quietly.

"Sure, how about we shop together after you get off work and we can make dinner together?"

"Okay. That'll work."

"Great!" Henry was relieved. Things were okay then. "Can I have a sweet roll and a cup of coffee?"

"Yeah, sure."

Henry took his order over to the table and sat down. It was going to be okay. She was making him crazy though. He sat quietly, trying not to watch her. He knew that if he got the angle right, he could watch her reflection in the big front window. He could discreetly watch her. She seemed to be ignoring him.

Naomi Blue

Naomi, however, was not ignoring Henry. As he looked out the window, not even talking to her for a change, she watched him. He seemed so at ease with himself, sitting with his coffee, looking out at the street. She appreciated his calmness, something she did not particularly feel.

Naomi was torn. The pattern of her life in Copper Prairie had been fine. She worked at the bakery, she window modeled, she took care of Beatrix, and most mornings she made her bed. For months she had been fine. Although she knew rationally she ought to be involved with people in town, she felt more comfortable, safer even, when she didn't. Her relationships were fine, but not of any depth. Except for Henry. And it was because of her involvement with him that she felt uneasy. Relationships led to hurt so often, even when they began so sweetly. Men are wonderful when they love you and destructive when they cheat. And Henry was simply too young. She had so much trouble getting around that. Her fortieth birthday was in a week, and it loomed. It wasn't that she minded turning forty, but she worried that the birthday—the absolute number of her years—would make Henry realize that she was too old for him. She was preparing herself for this, she knew, by keeping her distance from him.

But now they had plans for the evening. She didn't want to be distant, but she was nervous. She was completely attracted to Henry. She loved being with him. His easygoing nature balanced her worries and insecurities. And so far, the years between them had not seemed to be an issue. But what if she were forty?

He suddenly looked at her, as if he knew she was thinking about him. She turned away quickly, embarrassed. Aha, she could see how much he cared, despite pretending to be cool about it. She too felt the attraction. It was physical, most definitely, but it wasn't only physical. She enjoyed being near him, even when they were just walking Beatrix together. She liked watching him sit there. She liked to do anything at all with him. She was even beginning to enjoy his quite obvious obsession with watching her model.

She couldn't wait to be off work.

Henry Alexander

The rest of the afternoon had crawled by for Henry. He'd gone home after having coffee at Ida's Bakery and showered for the second time in the day. He stretched out on his futon to relax by watching the news and then C-SPAN. The after-election coverage was boring, and he drifted into a light sleep.

When he woke up, he knew instantly he had to hurry. The sun was beginning to set earlier in the evening, and his apartment had darkened. Naomi had agreed to meet him at Robinson's Grocery at 4:30, when she got off work. It wouldn't be good to be late.

Naomi was there when he walked in. She was carrying a basket and had already put in some apples, cheese and an assortment box of crackers.

"Hi, Naomi."

"Hi. I started without you. I hope that's okay."

Henry smiled and walked alongside Naomi as they talked through their menu and what they each knew how to prepare. Henry wasn't surprised to realize that she didn't particularly know how to cook. However, he had a few meals he'd mastered over the years, primarily to impress women who came over on dates. They were meals meant to make him look less like a guy who'd grown up with hot dish four times a week (and leftovers the other three days). He was most proud that none of his recipes used canned ingredients. He made a Thai-style beef with vegetables, spicy chicken with rice, and really excellent sloppy joes. None of the meals were fancy, but he could prepare them without a cookbook. He figured that three dishes would get him past the opening stages of a relationship, beyond which he was going to win a girl over with more than his cooking skills. Henry didn't see this as shallow, but rather, as vital dating know-how. Walking through Robinson's, he casually suggested the chicken and rice dish and Naomi agreed that it sounded good.

Back at Naomi Blue's house, Henry was glad to take the lead in cooking dinner. Naomi was kept busy hunting down the right tools.

"Do you have a cutting board anywhere?"

"What about a sharp knife?"

"Any chance you have a carrot scraper?"

She spent a lot of time sliding open drawers and rummaging around until she found something that would work. Henry was surprised by the sparseness of her kitchen. Over the years, he had ended up with at least one of everything. She barely had one of anything.

With dinner simmering on the stove finally, Henry and Naomi sat down at the kitchen table. Naomi seemed ill at ease. Her eyes flitted around, landing anywhere but on him. Henry leaned back in his chair, hoping to relax Naomi with his own body language. Naomi leaned back as well.

"So, Naomi, how does it feel to be sitting in your kitchen with a city elder?"

She laughed. "I think it's cool that you won the election. It's also a little funny. I can't wait until you officially take office. You'll look like such a baby with all those old men. I think I'll need to go to your swearing in. Do they actually swear you in?"

"I think so. I haven't gotten that far. I've been given a bunch of stuff to read to prepare me. There's a lot to learn. I thought I knew Copper Prairie pretty well, but I've never looked at it from this vantage point. It's really different. Bond ratings, community development, and budgets—I really have no experience in any of those things. I hardly know what a bond rating is."

Beatrix came up to Henry and put her snout on his thigh. Henry scratched the dog's head, causing her tail to wag furiously. It didn't take much to make this dog happy.

"She likes you," Naomi told him.

"Good."

Naomi became quiet. Henry let the silence grow. She wasn't always easy to understand. Her moods seemed to swing on matters that he had not yet figured out.

"So, did you know it's my birthday on Sunday?" Naomi asked.

"Really? This Sunday?"

"Yup."

"What birthday? How old will you be?"

"It's a big birthday."

"How big?"

Naomi said nothing. She went over to the stove.

"No! Don't open that lid," Henry admonished her. "The rice won't be happy."

Naomi dramatically lifted both hands away from the pan.

"How big?" he asked again.

"Big."

"Come here, Naomi."

She stayed where she was.

"Come on." Henry opened his arms. To his surprise, she came over and gingerly sat on his leg. "Aw, Naomi, don't worry so much." He wrapped his arms around her, pulling her close.

"It's a big birthday, Henry."

"So what. I don't care how old you are."

"You might."

"I don't."

"Forty."

Henry didn't say a word, hoping to avoid saying something that might make Naomi react or get up. He loved having her so close. But forty was up there. It sounded old. She was probably as close to his parents' age as she was to his age. That was weird. He held her tight to him. Even as he reacted inside to her age, he also knew that it didn't change a thing.

"So what," he said. "What does that matter? And why would it matter all of sudden now?"

"It sounds old, I think. Doesn't it? Forty is when I was supposed to be married with kids, making retirement plans, or owning a kayak or something. I should have savings, a 401(k) or something. Isn't forty middle aged? It's just, it's just not how I see myself. It's not where I am yet."

Henry listened. He was pretty good at listening to women, and had learned that there were times, mostly when they were sharing insecurities, that being quiet, physically supporting, with an even open expression was probably more important than challenging their assumptions or trying to fix their problems. It was a strategy that had worked in the past. When the woman had talked it out, he would then respond. Henry also wanted to avoid saying the wrong thing because he had yet to tackle thirty and couldn't quite imagine forty. He let her talk.

"I have been worried that we're at different places in our lives, that you will think 'forty?' and go running. I'm worried that maybe I'm too old for you, too old and fat and saggy."

"Naomi. I think maybe you've got two things going on in your head. One is that you are worried about my reaction to your age and the other is you are reacting to your own concept of what forty is."

He realized that she had begun to cry. He'd never seen Naomi Blue cry before. He figured he had accurately summarized her feelings. He kept holding her on his lap, stroking her back, her hair. He waited a bit before saying more, letting her relax.

"Naomi, I don't care about your age. And I don't care about any notion of what you should or should not have accomplished by this age. For god's sake, look at me. I'm certainly not on any proper path to success." His hand worked its way down the length of her braid. He pulled out the band at the bottom and began to weave his fingers up through the braided hair, undoing the braid. She held still. Her crying seemed to have eased. She shifted her weight slightly on his lap, but said nothing. He continued to gently unbraid her hair with his fingers. She shifted again. And as her hair was finally free from the braid, he stopped thinking altogether and kissed her. They slid together from the chair rather ungracefully onto the floor. Beatrix jumped at the sudden motion and then curled into a ball a couple of feet away and lowered her lids, watching Henry and Naomi take off the minimum amount of clothes necessary to make love on the cold linoleum floor.

"Naomi, none of that matters," Henry said softly. Naomi murmured something in reply into his neck that he wasn't even sure were words. They stayed like that until the smell of burning rice caused them to jump up in an attempt at saving supper.

SEBASTIAN SKINNER

BEATRIX'S POOR HEARING AND EXCELLENT ABILITY to fall into a rabbit-chasing sleep on a moment's notice made her an ineffective watchdog. Mostly, she watched Naomi Blue. While Henry and Naomi were immersed in the kitchen, dusk had fallen, and Sebastian Skinner was not having a focused sort of day. He had found the note he had last written to Wanda still in his pocket and was confused why he hadn't yet delivered it. He put a small flashlight in his pocket and once again began to walk down the tracks. It was a cold evening and dark because the moon had not yet risen. But Sebastian knew those tracks and was only thinking of one thing—delivering the note.

When he got to her house, he carefully came down from the tracks into the yard. He'd get the key and put the note into the Meyer's Landing birdhouse, the one Lyle had built from the old dock they had torn down shortly after the war, trying to make some extra money. Lyle had wanted all the salvageable wood, saying it was already weathered perfectly for birdhouses. Sebastian had wanted to haul it away in his pickup and leave it at the dump, but Lyle wanted it neatly piled in his yard where he could use it, taking out the remaining screws and bolts that held the dock together originally. Sebastian complained about the time it took to bring all the old wood to Lyle's house and help pull nails and screws from it. Sebastian never told Lyle that he thought those were amazingly beautiful birdhouses, some of the nicest he'd ever made. But those birdhouses sure sold like crazy at the Copper Crafts Show that July. Wanda had prettily sat there in her red and white polka dotted blouse and white slacks and sold them all, with small paper American flags poking out from the chimneys. He had bought one himself just to be near Wanda, just to have the chance to lean over the table to pick out the birdhouse he wanted, getting close enough to smell her perfume.

Lyle had not joined her at the table. He didn't care at all about selling birdhouses. He was simply devoted to making them. He made each one different from the next, the roofline angled differently, the doorway arched not square, or with metal pegs or old branches for perches. Sebastian didn't know where Lyle got his ideas, but he created works of art. Lyle did not want any of them. Not a one. He didn't mind Wanda making a little money selling them, but he wanted nothing to do with it. Lyle said he built them because he liked to keep his hands busy, that it kept him from playing cards too much and losing money to Sebastian. He said it kept his mind steady. And when he was building out in the garage, Wanda would not bother him. Lyle would turn on the radio, listening to polka music from a local radio station. And he built birdhouse after birdhouse.

Wanda loved them. She said they made her dream. Their imperfections made them perfect. The old barns, fences or docks made each one a piece of history. Each one was a part of another life, someone else's life. They were individual with their rough-hewn edges, sometimes with shingle roofs, sometimes with upstairs windows. Her passion for the houses made no sense to Sebastian, but she saved the ones she loved most, storing them in the backyard shed.

Not long after that day that he saw her reach into the birdhouse on the crab tree, he tried it himself. Lyle was at the city elder meeting, and Wanda used to like to go along and listen to the men deliberate about the town. It was her civic duty, she thought, to attend their meetings. Sebastian typically went too, just to have the chance to visit with Wanda, but that summer evening, he went to their house instead. He reached into the birdhouse and found the key to the shed. The key was hot in his hands, he recalled, as if it were only a day ago. Guilt and excitement filled him as he opened the lock on the shed door. He knew she kept the birdhouses, but was surprised to see them stacked high in the shed. A mess. They were balanced precariously, one on top of the other. No order. No sense of balance. The mess made Sebastian uneasy. He locked the shed up, returned the key to the birdhouse on the crab tree, and arrived forty-five minutes late to the city elder meeting.

Two weeks later, during the next city elder meeting, he returned armed with a hammer and a box of nails. He organized the dozens of birdhouses in the shed, neatly arranging them on the walls like a puzzle. She would be surprised. He loved her. She would see that. She would know that. He put a note in one of the birdhouses, just the edge sticking out.

"My love. I live so close yet so apart from what matters to me. Living with the absence of words and the silence of touch. I long for more."

Sebastian had then stayed away from Wanda and Lyle's house for a long time after that. He was fearful that she might be furious. But Wanda herself had come into his store three weeks later. He had kept himself busy in the men's clothing while she shopped. Finally, it would have been rude to avoid her any longer and he decided to treat her like any other customer. She was slipping her feet into a pair of suede pumps, bending over for the other one when he pulled up the shoe-fitting bench in front of her. "May I?" he had asked. She had pointed her foot out and he held it in his hands for a long moment before easing her left foot into the shoe.

"Thank you," she smiled at him. Wanda never mentioned the birdhouses.

Chapter Twenty-One

Ida Minsky

Finally, there could be no doubt that it was winter. Snow that began before Election Day continued through November. The ground had frozen solid and likely wouldn't thaw until late April. Ida was glad that she had no need to drive during the harsh Minnesota winters. The snow might affect business, but she could manage the slow days.

Ida was taking wheat rolls out of the oven when Naomi Blue came in. Ida glanced at the clock and was pleased to see that she was one minute early. The girl had been her best hire ever, she thought.

"Hi, Mrs. Minsky," Naomi said, wiping her boots on the mat and taking off her sweater.

"Yes, hello, Naomi. Hello." Ida kept to her work and eyed Naomi as she put on her apron and washed her hands.

"What is new with you and the boy?" Ida hadn't planned on saying this and such a question was out of character. She tried to be discreet and respect her employee's privacy. But she was curious and found the two of them an odd match, although one she liked. It must be true that opposites attract. Naomi didn't answer. Had she heard? Ida pulled out another tray of rolls and set them on a rack to cool. Maybe it was indeed too rude a question to ask.

"Well, nothing really," Naomi finally responded. "I mean, we are kind of still dating, and it's going okay, I guess."

"You sound so wishy-washy."

"I don't know. I'm just not certain about this whole thing. He's so much younger . . ."

"So? What's the matter with that?"

"I don't know. And I'm really stressed out because it's my birthday tomorrow, and I'll be forty. Forty. I don't think he'll be too eager to be with a forty-year-old woman. Do you?"

"Why not?"

"Well. I don't know." Naomi's voice trailed off.

"I think you're worrying about the wrong things. If he loves you, he'll love you if you're forty."

"I guess." Naomi didn't sound too sure of this. Ida decided to change the subject.

"How is your modeling job going?"

Naomi laughed. "I'm not much of a model. All I do is dress up and stand there. It's kind of boring, but at least I get new clothes out of the deal."

"Is Mr. Skinner easy to work for?"

"Well, he's a little odd, I think. Sometimes he forgets I'm in the window, and when I come out, he looks at me really strangely. I don't quite know what's going on with him. He is pretty old."

"He's older than forty," Ida said chuckling under her breath.

"Way older. But he's nice enough. And he loves to pick out clothes for me to model in. When I come in he seems to get this rush of energy and runs around the store grabbing clothes for me to wear."

"Hmph. Sounds like Sebastian."

"He's a gentleman, though, Mrs. Minsky. Don't get me wrong. He's just a little odd."

Ida thought the whole arrangement a little odd.

"Are you still, um, seeing Mr. Robinson?" Naomi asked.

Hah, thought Ida, *there's the problem with asking personal questions. They get reciprocated. I should know better than to get myself into this kind of conversation*, she thought.

"Yes, Mr. Robinson and I are still seeing each other. It has become very comfortable. I like him quite a bit. So, now, let's get back to work, yes?" Not only was it more than she wanted to say about her relationship, but more than she had ever said aloud to anybody about her relationship. That was plenty. And of course, it wasn't really the truth either. Her relationship with Rooster Robinson was comfortable, yes, but it was more than that. It was exciting. She actually wanted him to spend the night. She wanted him to explore the boundaries of her nightgown. She wanted him there for dinner. She wanted him there in the morning. She remembered that first time he sat across from her for tea, and she looked at him in that objective way, noticing his age, his hairiness, his lack of grooming, his rough ways. She had wondered if she could look at that man day in and day out. Now when she sat across from him, those very same things were still true—not a single hair had been snipped and not a single manner had improved. But she didn't care. They simply didn't matter. She noticed them, but she accepted them as the man.

She hoped the day would go quickly. The bakery was still of the utmost importance to her, but so was her time upstairs in her apartment.

Naomi Blue

Naomi was pleased that her ploy to have Ida Minsky talk about her and Rooster had worked. But after all, it was fair after Ida had asked about her relationship with Henry. She was pleased with her strategy.

It was a slow day at the bakery, and Naomi had time to brood about her birthday. She wouldn't have it, she decided. She'd just make it an ordinary day. She and Henry had not made plans for it and that was just as well. Tomorrow was the one day she didn't want to see him. If she could just skip over the day, it would be better.

Before she left, she asked Ida for the next day off, saying she had big plans for her birthday. Ida had smiled slyly and said of course she could have the day off. Of course.

Chapter Twenty-Two

Sebastian Skinner

Sebastian woke up the next morning and felt irritable. He got up and went into the bathroom. He used the toilet and brushed his teeth. Still in his flannel pajamas, he went down the hall into the kitchen. Dishes had piled up in the sink. A faded red plastic drying rack next to the sink stood empty. Yes, it was time to clean the dishes. But he didn't feel like it. He drank a glass of water.

He walked to the refrigerator where a calendar hung on the side, still turned to November. A magnet held a few photos on the refrigerator door. Nieces and nephews he had only met once or twice hung beside five colorful drawings from Miss Markus' second grade class who had come to the Carriage General for a tour. Such silliness, he had thought, but he'd been touched by the thank-you crayon drawings the children had sent. Some were in the back of the store, and these five hung here. Miss Markus had looked too young to be a teacher, but she had assured him that she had her degree from Hamline University in St. Paul.

One of Wanda and Lyle's sons had become a teacher too and was living down in Missouri or Iowa, he couldn't recall. He had gone to a graduation party, or was it a wedding, and they had put a tent up in the backyard for the event. A tent the size of the yard, and it had rained like mad, and everyone kept saying how good it was that they had the tent, but it dripped on the edges and everyone got wet anyway.

He opened the drawer that held his writing materials. He needed to write a note to Wanda. He needed to tell her. He needed to let her know. And just like so many other mornings over the past fifty or more years, Sebastian wrote a love note to Wanda. He knew just the birdhouse he would put it in. Just the one. In the far right corner, up near the roof, was a large white stained house, quite stately. That was the one he'd put the note in. He needed to get going.

Sebastian Skinner slid his feet into his big black boots and slung his arms into his coat, putting the note in the chest pocket. He began the familiar trek down the railroad tracks. The wind was ferocious, and he felt in his pockets for his cap. Not there. Too late now, he thought. He'd get down to the house, open the shed, hide the note and be gone. Quick as can be. Home before he knew it.

He walked halfway down the tracks with his hands cupped around his ears. They were nearly frozen. *Be quick about it,* he thought. Get going. He didn't understand why walking on the tracks had become so damned hard. He kept going.

Naomi Blue

Naomi loved the laziness of a day off. Beatrix was already on the bed, pressing into her. If Naomi wasn't careful, she might fall off as the dog took over more bed real estate. She tried hard not to move so the dog wouldn't know she was awake.

She remembered. It's today. She had loved birthdays growing up, loved the parties and the cake and the presents. With Will, birthdays had become a time of unmet expectations. Had she been unrealistic wanting him to surprise her with a special gift or a night out or a party? Was that too much to have hoped for? Maybe it was. He would ask her what she wanted and she would say she didn't know. All she wanted was for him to decide, to know her well enough to get her something, without her making a list. Surprise me, she'd say. It's the thought that counts. And finally, the day would come, and Will would hand her a card with a long note. It's the thought that counts, right, he would ask innocently. Of course, she'd say and sulk away. It is the thought, but I really wanted a gift, something from you. Don't have expectations, she would admonish herself. Other holidays would come and this pattern would repeat. Yet she would have spent days planning the most special gift for him, a surprise, the unexpected, and then she would make a big deal out of it. So now, she was under the covers, breathing her own hot breath, listening to the half snore of Beatrix, thinking of how much more relaxed this was.

Maybe Henry would remember her birthday. Hopefully not. But it didn't matter. She expected nothing. She touched her stomach. Did it feel forty? Her legs. Her breasts. The back of her arms. *Is this what forty feels like? It isn't so bad. Okay, happy birthday, Naomi.*

Sebastian Skinner

SEBASTIAN PULLED THE BRANCH DOWN on the crab apple and reached inside. Where was that damned key? He fished around the small opening, his fingers nearly too frozen to feel anything. It wasn't in there. What had she done with it? Had Wanda moved it? Where could it possibly be? He went over to the shed. The lock was still there. He jiggled it to see if perhaps the lock hadn't quite caught. One day, he had come to the shed to find the lock completely off. He'd slowly opened the door. Wanda was sitting in the rocking chair facing away from the door. She'd rocked back abruptly, startled by the light from outside. He'd quickly told her it was just he and he'd come inside the shed pulling shut the door. He had kneeled in front of her, pulling her forward in the chair. She had not said a word. Nothing. Just let him stroke her hair, her shoulders, and kiss her quickly but purposefully. He had forgotten to give her the note that day. No luck today, though, it was locked. What did that mean? Why would Wanda have locked him out of the shed? He was beginning to shake with cold. Should've worn a hat. Damn, it's cold this morning. He leaned against the shed.

The ache he began to feel was as much emotional as it was physical. The cold was seeping through his coat into his bones. His ears and nose were numb. He shoved his hands in his pockets. He felt the note. Wanda. He had to give her the note. Why was the shed locked? Where was the key? Wanda. I love her, even if she is playing hard to get. Wanda. Where did you put that damned key?

Sebastian stumbled and fell to his knees in the snow. *For God's sake*, he thought, *what am I doing in the snow? Get up, you old man, or you'll freeze to death out here and Lyle will find you. He'll ask why you're out at the shed. Get up. Where was Lyle? He must be at the city elder meeting. Yes, of course. He would simply go up to the house and give Wanda the note himself. Why not?* Surely she would understand. Warm him up. Give him a cup of tea. He stood up and went to the back door and banged.

NAOMI BLUE

B<small>EATRIX WAS GOING MAD</small>. She had jumped off the bed and was tearing downstairs barking, her claws scratching and slipping down the wooden steps. She was crazy. Naomi was nervous. The dog had never done this before.

She heard banging. The back door. Someone was there. Must be Henry. Why was he at the back? A birthday surprise?

She threw on the pair of jeans and a sweatshirt she'd flung on the chair the night before. She relaxed. Henry was always surprising her with something. She hoped it wasn't another birdcage or a bird. She decided he could wait a little longer as she pulled on a pair of rag wool socks. He would just have to be patient.

Beatrix's barking was insistent as Naomi went down the stairs. She could hear the dog's claws up on the back door. Something sure had her going. "Get down, Beatrix, down," she said as she peeked out the window before opening the door.

Sebastian Skinner literally fell into the room. She reached out to steady his arm, but he was already in full motion towards the floor. Sebastian was clattering. It took Naomi a few seconds to realize it was his teeth. She had never heard teeth make that noise before except on early morning cartoons.

"Mr. Skinner!" she cried. "Are you okay?"

Sebastian fell onto his side, curled into a mess of boots and coat. As he coat slipped open, she could see flannel pajamas underneath and nothing else. A bit of bare chest with gray scraggly hair peeked out from where a button had popped off his top. What was he doing in just pajamas?

"Wait here!" she exclaimed and ran upstairs and grabbed a blanket off her bed to cover him with. Keep him warm, raise his body temperature. His lips were oddly blue and his teeth were still making that horrible noise. Naomi called 911.

The call was automatically routed to the police station where Officer Millerton was reorganizing his office. He had been contemplating whether his desk should face the window or the door and had moved his heavy steel file cabinets to the other side of the small room to make the switch. The phone startled him. The emergency line didn't ring often, and at first, he wondered if it was a prank. More often than not, calls were for squirrels in the attic or public inebriation outside the Ringworm. This time, it appeared it was no prank. That woman living in the Coopers' house was frantic and talking in a high-pitched voice. He heard the words "frozen" and "help" and "Sebastian Skinner." As Office Millerton started the engine of his Ford pickup, he tried to piece those words together to determine the nature of the emergency. He raced down to the Cooper's house.

A barking dog wasn't his favorite greeting on an emergency call, but Naomi Blue met him at the door, too, and rushed him back to the kitchen. Sure enough, Sebastian Skinner was stretched out on her linoleum kitchen floor, a floral blanket over him and his head on a potholder.

"Mr. Skinner," Officer Millerton said gently, kneeling beside the man. "Are you okay?" He felt for his pulse. He was definitely alive, but cold, and his pulse slow. "Sebastian."

Slowly, Sebastian Skinner opened his eyes. "Wanda?" he asked. "Wanda?"

Officer Millerton looked at Naomi Blue. Naomi Blue raised her eyebrows in confusion. Sebastian looked at Naomi. He weakly lifted his hand, and she took it. It was so cold. She let his hand warm between both of hers. He released the note into her hand and closed his eyes.

Office Millerton called for the Copper Prairie Volunteer Ambulance Squad, though it would likely take them twenty minutes to arrive, since it was early morning and many of them were probably not yet up and about. Sebastian was beginning to warm up, and Officer Millerton stayed beside him. Naomi got up and went into the living room to watch for the ambulance and for some privacy to read the note.

"Wanda. I dream of you when I close my eyes in the day, like snowflakes through my mind images of you float softly. I hear you whisper to me and imagine my hands against your cheek. My yearning remains constant and everlasting. I pray you will come back to me. I love you. Only you. My sweet."

This was the same handwriting as the notes in the birdhouses. So it was Sebastian Skinner who wrote the poems and notes. It was Sebastian Skinner who loved Wanda Cooper. It was beginning to make sense. She slipped the note into her pocket and went back to the kitchen.

"Wanda. Please." Sebastian was more alert, but clearly confused.

"Should I make him some tea?" she asked Officer Millerton. "Can he sit up?"

"We can try." As Naomi put water on to boil, Officer Millerton helped Sebastian Skinner to sit up, propping him against the wall for support.

"I'm so cold, Wanda, so cold."

"I have tea for you." Naomi brought over a small mug of tea. She held it to his lips. He sipped it noisily while looking at Naomi.

"Ah . . . good. Thank you. Thank you so much, Wanda."

Naomi was uncomfortable. There was that look again. As if he was looking at someone else. She must be Wanda Cooper to him. He was confused. It was easier to play along. She was glad Officer Millerton didn't say anything about it, although he had cocked his head oddly at her, and she knew she was right to play along.

The ambulance arrived soon and lifted Sebastian from her floor onto a stretcher, wrapping him carefully in thin white blankets to warm him up further. They took him out the front.

Officer Millerton, however, did not leave.

"How did Sebastian Skinner come to be in your kitchen, Miss Blue?" He held his notebook with his pen poised to record her answer.

"I don't really know. I mean, I heard a banging on my back door, and there he was, half frozen to death."

"Why did he come here this morning?"

"I don't know. He's never come to my house before."

"I see. Why do you think he came to your house today?"

"I have no idea."

Naomi was not certain that Officer Millerton believed her, or maybe that was just the way policemen question people. Either way, she didn't care for his tone.

"What is the nature of your relationship with Mr. Skinner?"

"We have no relationship!" Naomi bristled.

"Let me restate that, Miss Blue. How do you know Mr. Skinner?"

"I work for him once a week. I model for him."

"You model for him? Um." Now Office Millerton was uncomfortable. His mind raced. She modeled for him?

"Yes, I model at the store. In the store window. I window model."

"Ah, I see." Officer Millerton was trying to understand. What was a window model exactly?

"I stand in some of his clothes and model, standing totally still in the window. Like a manikin."

"You wear his clothes?"

"Not *his* clothes. Clothes from the store!" Naomi wasn't sure if this guy was quite as dense as he sounded.

After a few more questions and some rapid flipping through his pages of notes, Officer Millerton told her that he thought he had all he needed and left.

Naomi picked up the potholder and wondered if it needed washing. This was a strange start to a birthday.

Ida Minsky

Ida and Rooster Robinson were sleeping late. When Ida finally woke up, she slid her feet into slippers and went quietly downstairs to put a note on the door saying the bakery was closed for the day. When she got back upstairs, she could hear Roger's gentle snoring. She pulled her nightgown over her head, dropped it on the small braided rug, and shivering, got back under the pile of quilts beside Roger. His snoring stopped. She lay on her side facing him. As he reached his arm out to bring her closer to him, he discovered her unexpected nakedness. Ida held her breath. She usually acted as if she was less than interested in the physical aspect of their relationship, as if she were allowing him to have her. This was the first time she had made such an effort, to show interest, to offer herself in such a way. He kept his eyes closed as she ran her hand down the length of him, finding him, and she shivered again in the realization of what she could make happen. Still with his eyes closed, Roger shifted Ida beneath him and with some effort, began to move within her. Some moments later, it was the unusual sound of an ambulance siren that caused Roger to stop moving and open his eyes. Their faces only inches apart and neither unable to focus at so close a range, they stared at each other. Neither spoke. Neither moved. As the sound of the siren receded out of town, Roger rested his head next to Ida's ear.

"I love you," he whispered. "I'm sure of it."

Ida tightened her arms around his back and whispered back, "Yes. I'm sure of it too."

Henry Alexander

The night before had not been one of Henry's best. After avoiding the bars for a week, he had gone into the Ringworm for a beer. One turned to three and then another two just to be social and for the first time in a long time, he danced with strangers to a country western band. It wasn't his kind of music, but once he got going, it didn't seem to matter one way or another.

This morning he was paying the price with a headache and unsettled stomach. He slept as long as he could, hoping to wake up feeling better. The sound of a siren screaming past his apartment set him on edge. He drank a large glass of water and tried to get moving. It simply wasn't going to happen, so he shut his eyes again. It felt better not to move. The phone rang. Was it Sunday? He tried to speak with his parents regularly on Sundays, and they loved to call him early. It was as if they were checking up on him.

He rolled over with a groan and picked up the phone. But it wasn't his mother at all. It was Naomi Blue. Naomi rarely called him, and he tried to rise to the occasion, making his voice sound more chipper than he felt.

He hung up the phone and rolled onto his back, pulling the pillow over his face. It was hard to concentrate on what she had said. Sebastian Skinner had come to her house in his pajamas, fallen into her arms as cold as an ice cube, then Office Millerton came after Naomi called 911, Sebastian had given her a love note, and it was her birthday. He presumed this made sense, but his brain could not find the logic in any part of it. The birthday part woke him up. Yes, today was Naomi's birthday. He had forgotten. After all their talk about the "big one," it was here, and he had forgotten. It would be hard to explain to her that her fortieth birthday meant so little to him that he actually forgot it. That was sure to get him in hot water; one just doesn't forget one's girlfriend's birthday. But in truth, her turning forty hadn't bothered him. Okay, Hank, you don't need to tell her you forgot. It's her birthday. Today. You forgot. No present. Nothing. You slug. You jerk. You moron. You forgot. He thought he ought to get up and crawl his tired body over to the Carriage General and get her a present. But Sebastian Skinner had been at her house half naked and left by ambulance. Wouldn't that mean the store would be closed? You're sunk, he thought. You've totally screwed this up. He shut his eyes again.

Eventually, Henry got up and took a shower, letting the steamy water cleanse him of the prior night. Nothing was simple with a hangover.

He walked past the Carriage General seeing that it was indeed closed. Then he went down to Ida's Bakery. He needed a birthday cake. Ida's was dark, the "closed" sign facing the street. What was going on today, he wondered. Where was everyone? He needed a cake. He knocked on the door, despite the fact that he couldn't see anyone in the bakery. He knocked harder. He peered inside. Nobody. He knocked again. His head ached making so much noise, but he seemed to have lost all rational thought. He needed a cake for Naomi.

IDA MINSKY

IDA SIMPLY WASN'T THE KIND OF PERSON to stay in bed late. She wasn't used to being idle. Now Roger was snoring again. For some reason, it bothered her this morning. After making love, he had gone straight back to sleep while she was fully awake. How could that happen? Then she heard a knocking. It was barely discernible at first over the sound of Rooster's snorts and deep breaths. But eventually, it became distinct and repetitive. Now what? That man can sleep through anything, she thought. She got out of bed and quickly dressed. The banging downstairs didn't cease.

Ida went down the staircase and into the darkened bakery. She could see immediately who it was. The boy. Naomi Blue's boy. She turned the deadbolt and opened the door.

"What is it? What's the emergency? Why are you banging on my door? Can't you see I'm closed?"

"Yes, yes," he muttered. "Thank you, thank you for opening up. I need you."

Ida started to laugh. The poor boy.

"I need a cake, Mrs. Minsky. It's Naomi Blue's birthday. It's her fortieth birthday. Today. And I need a cake. Today."

"I'm closed. You saw that?"

"Yes, but it's for Naomi."

"Hmph. Well, okay. I can bake her a cake. Yes, she's forty today. Okay. What kind of cake do you want?"

"Chocolate. No, make it vanilla. Vanilla with chocolate frosting. And some roses on top or something."

"Let's get started."

"Let's?"

"You keep me company. You stay and keep me company while we get this in the oven and then no charge."

"Okay," Henry said. "How can I help?"

"Just keep me company. I don't think you look too well. Are you feeling okay?"

"Not really."

"Okay, I will make us some coffee and get started."

And so Henry pulled a chair into the kitchen, drank black coffee and watched Ida Minsky create a cake. He leaned on his elbows, his head apparently too heavy to keep up without their help. Ida smelled the residue of alcohol coming from him, and although she would have liked to tease him, decided to spare him the embarrassment. Clearly he was suffering already.

"Henry," she said, sliding the sheet cake into the oven. "I have an idea. Why don't we have a little party here in the bakery later this afternoon? We can surprise Naomi. I'll get her here. You round up some friends. I will too. And we can have a party." She opened a drawer and pulled out a package of multicolored birthday candles. "Yes?"

Henry's face brightened. "Yes! That's a great idea, Mrs. Minsky. How will you get her here?"

"Not a problem, not a problem. I'll call her in on a personnel matter. She'll come, I'm sure of that."

With their plans finalized, Henry went home presumably to make some calls to friends but also, Ida was sure, to go back to sleep. While the cake was cooling, she went back upstairs to see if Roger were awake. Perhaps she could get back into bed for a bit as well.

Naomi Blue

Naomi was drinking coffee at her kitchen table trying to make sense of the morning so far. One thing she now knew. It was Sebastian Skinner who had written those notes to Wanda Cooper. But had they been involved in a secret affair? How did the notes get into the shed? And what about the birdhouses? Who made them? Why were they there? Did Sebastian build the birdhouses and bring them to Wanda as gifts, with the notes hidden inside? What part did Lyle Cooper play in all of this? Things made more sense, but the pieces still didn't fit together.

The phone rang. *Ah, I bet this is Dorrie and Ronnie calling to wish me happy birthday*, Naomi thought. The thought of listening to that slightly delayed connection from Costa Rica, their off-tune voices, and the added depressive fact that she was sitting there alone on her birthday, made her not answer the phone. There was great control in not answering a ringing phone, Naomi felt. But when it rang again, she answered it, knowing how little control she had.

But it wasn't her mother calling. It was Ida Minsky and she didn't sound too happy. She asked her to stop by the bakery at three o'clock to discuss her employment terms. Employment terms? That didn't sound promising. Was she being fired? She couldn't think of a good reason for Ida to fire her. She was usually on time. And she hadn't broken any dishes or been rude to customers. Maybe she would need to step up her hours modeling instead. There weren't too many options in town.

Naomi Blue hung up the phone unnerved. The phone rang again. Answer it? Why not.

"Hello?"

There it was. Her mother and Ronnie singing. She laughed, realizing they were singing in Spanish. Some headway in their language classes had been made apparently.

"Feliz birthday. Happy birthday. How are you darling?"

"Fine, I'm fine. Thanks for singing."

"How's the weather in Minnesota? We've got a gorgeous day here. Hot, though it's been raining in the afternoons. So much rain. The road down to the beach is washing out. But it's still warm. We love Costa Rica. You ought to come down soon."

Her mother could keep a conversation going just fine without much input from Naomi. They talked more about the weather, the brittle cold of northern Minnesota and the humid sultriness of Latin America. Her mother promised a birthday card and check were on their way, but you know how slow the mail is down there. And soon, there was nothing more to say. Naomi hung up the phone and felt oddly disengaged.

Forty stank.

Sebastian Skinner

Sebastian Skinner was sitting in the hospital foyer in an irritated frame of mind. He was absolutely fine. He thought this was entirely obvious. He was completely fine. He had just gotten cold on his walk and now he was fine and happy to be leaving the hospital. The emergency room doctor claimed that he had been dehydrated, and his core temperature had dropped, causing a confused state. Sure he was cold, but he doubted hydration was his problem, but the damn hospital was certain that fluids and blankets were what a man needed to feel like himself again. It wasn't what he needed. Not at all what he needed. Nevertheless, he felt himself again.

As he sat waiting for Rooster Robinson to pick him up, he thought about what they called his "confused state." They had sent in a shrink, of all things, a shrink to ask him personal questions. Her nametag said MAGGIE SWENSEN, SOCIAL WORKER, but he knew she was really a shrink. He wondered if her grandfather could have been that accordian player from Chisholm, the bald Swede Swensen who nevertheless had a long thin greasy ponytail. But she was so serious, so intent on asking him a series of questions listed on her clipboard, he didn't ask her. He told her that he didn't need a social worker. He had snapped at her, telling her that he worked and was plenty social. She had laughed, irritating him further. He thought her questions were rude. She wanted to know what year it was, why Sebastian thought he was in the emergency room, how he came to be in his pajamas in the middle of winter at a stranger's house and if he lived alone. He became angry towards this Maggie Swensen, despite the possibility that Swede was her grandfather and told her that he was fine and enough was enough.

His confusion. Well, it was a bit unusual for him to walk down the tracks in his pajamas, but he had on his winter coat, so what was the problem? And it was Wanda's house he went to, not a stranger's, despite the fact that his model Naomi Blue lived there now. He knew that. Wanda had moved to Florida. He knew that. If the key hadn't been moved from the birdhouse, no one would have been the wiser. He just wanted to put the note in the birdhouse, after all. And so when he proclaimed his health and sanity, answering the questions adequately, the hospital let him go. He had called Rooster to give him a ride home. Rooster didn't ask him any questions on the phone and wasn't likely to pry. Thank goodness for old friends. But where the hell was he?

IDA MINSKY

B IRTHDAYS WEREN'T IDA MINSKY'S FAVORITE times either. She found it unsettling to think about her age. Even so, she didn't identify with Naomi Blue's unhappiness about turning forty. Naomi was so young. So much yet to happen. Ida's problem with her age was the sheer number of years behind her and the smaller number ahead. Yet these days with Rooster she felt a renewed sense of energy. It was crazy, she knew, that she actually felt younger. She had a sense of having something exciting to wake up to. Despite Rooster's stubbornness and external grouchiness, he was actually a sweet and gentle man. And Ida loved being with him.

When Ida was in her late twenties, her sister had asked her a simple question that had plagued her for years. If you could have the love of your life in the first third of your life, the middle third, or the latter third, which would you choose? Ida had pressed Rose. How long do I live? Can I only have one love in this scenario? Just one third of my life? And Rose had told her not to think so much but to just answer. So Ida had answered quickly and said she would want her true love when she was an old woman. Rose had been surprised. Rose was in love. Of course she was surprised. But then Ida had outlived her sister and that love, that true love, had not found Ida. It wasn't a matter of not loving, but a matter of not finding true love. In fact, Ida had long ago given up on such a possibility and even doubted the reality of it. But this thing with Rooster was moving swiftly in a direction she had little experience with. His company and friendship was warm, good and fun. The sex was caring and at times utterly passionate. But it was the constant thoughts she had about Roger Robinson that surprised her. Her own eagerness to see him, serve him a plate of cookies or feel him beside her in bed. It embarrassed her to admit that she felt beautiful for the first time in her life under his touch and kind eyes. He never mentioned her limp and didn't seem to mind her weight either. Maybe his vision was poor. Or maybe none of that mattered to him. And maybe she had simply gotten lucky in the last third of her life.

Henry Alexander

After a solid two hours of sleep, Henry woke up refreshed. It wasn't the refreshed feeling of a good night's sleep, but one where the moment you open your eyes you are aware that you have shed that headache and upset stomach. It's a tremendous sense of relief. It wasn't the first time that he decided that drinking this much was something he was not going to do again.

Although he felt better, he still needed to figure out something to give Naomi Blue for her birthday. With his favorite store closed, this wasn't going to be easy.

In desperation he went into the kitchen. Something useful and yet something clever. He knew there must be something he could give her. He opened a drawer. Rolling pin, tongs, spatula, grater, string to tie up a turkey. Nothing.

He pulled open his desk drawer and began rummaging through the odds and ends that had accumulated there. Paper clips, index cards, loose rubber bands and keys to unknown locations didn't give him any good ideas. Reaching in the back of the drawer he found the ideal gift—a beautiful well-worn blue quartz worry stone.

Naomi Blue

Naomi walked slowly to Ida's Bakery. She was worried about her job. She didn't want to lose it, and she didn't think her career in modeling had any promise. Despite her worries, she had decided that in honor of her birthday—and because she had yet to have any real reason to wear them—she would wear the teal cowboy boots. She tucked her jeans into the tops, creating a dramatic look, but if you couldn't wear crazy boots on your fortieth birthday, when could you. She was walking past the Ringworm when she realized that cowboy boots were a lousy choice in snow. She felt the loss of control well before she actually lost her footing, well before her left leg flew forward and all parts of her were airborne. Throwing her arm out to break her fall, she landed hard on her right wrist. She knew immediately by the distinct snapping sound that it must be broken. She didn't bother getting up. She laid her head back down on the sidewalk.

"Geez, that was quite a fall."

Naomi looked up into the face of Millie Bing. Naomi closed her eyes.

"Uh," Naomi said.

"Hey, you're really pale, Naomi. Are you okay?"

"My wrist is broken, I think. It hurts like hell."

"Okay, well, we all saw you go down from inside the bar. It was really a great move. Sit tight and we'll get you to the hospital."

"I don't need the hospital, just help me up."

"Yeah you do. At least get an x-ray and get it set if it's broken."

A friend of Millie's pulled his car up to the curb and Millie helped Naomi in, sliding in beside her.

"You don't need to come with me, Millie. You've done plenty already."

"Nah, I really haven't. Besides, I've been mad at you ever since I realized you were dating Hank. I know that's not really a good reason, but I thought, well . . . anyway, you didn't mention it when we talked about him that day."

"Oh."

"Man, you look really pale. Your wrist hurts, I bet."

"I guess. I'm sorry, Millie."

"Well, you could have told me you were dating him when I was going on and on about him."

"I wanted to but it didn't seem the right time or something. I don't want to get into it right now, if that's okay." Naomi Blue shut her eyes. She wasn't in the mood for this conversation and the smell of beer exuding from Millie was making her stomach turn.

Naomi sent Millie back to town, convincing her that she was fine on her own at the emergency room. The automatic doors swooshed open, and Naomi didn't turn back to say goodbye.

Sebastian Skinner

Sebastian was impatient waiting for Rooster to come get him. He knew Rooster would get there, but the smell of the hospital was beginning to bother him, and he wanted to get home. He really ought to open the store. Why wasn't Rooster here already?

And then she walked in. The girl. The curvy girl who was not Wanda. It was his model, his lovely window model, Naomi Blue, right before him. And she was wearing those ridiculous green-blue cowboy boots she got that first day after modeling. Those boots had sat in the discount bin gathering dust for a couple of years or more. Until she came, he was sure they would never leave the store. Naomi was holding her arm oddly in front of her.

"Naomi?" he called.

She turned to see who had called her name, her face ashen. "Mr. Skinner?"

"What happened to you? Why are you here? I'm waiting for Rooster Robinson to pick me up. Waitin' a long time. Why are you here?"

"I fell. I think my wrist is broken."

Sebastian got up from his chair, which wasn't particularly comfortable anyway, and helped her to the registration desk. She turned towards him, feeling his hand on the small of her back.

"Are you okay now, Mr. Skinner? That was crazy this morning."

"Yes, yes, I'm fine. Don't worry about me. Let's just get you taken care of."

"Sebastian!" Finally, there he was. Rooster had gotten off his lazy butt to pick him up. It was about time. The ornery feeling he'd been harboring waiting for Rooster had already begun to lighten as he sat beside Naomi. Naomi, not Wanda.

Sebastian stood up.

"What's going on? Why are you here with Naomi Blue? I thought I was giving you a ride home."

"You are, Rooster, you are. Just relax. Naomi broke her wrist, and I'm helping her here, can't you see that?"

"Ah, yes, I do see that." Rooster sounded doubtful and Sebastian figured he thought he was still confused.

And so it was that both Sebastian Skinner and Rooster Robinson accompanied Naomi Blue to the examination area, Sebastian sitting on a small fold out chair beside the examining table and Rooster leaning back against a tile wall, feeling uncomfortably large in the confined space.

The doctor was the same one who had examined Sebastian and he came in with a confused expression, seeing Sebastian still there and now Rooster as well.

"Don't ask," Sebastian said gruffly.

"Yeah, don't," Rooster agreed.

The doctor nodded and began to focus his attention on Naomi, who was clearly a patient in pain.

"Miss Blue, do you want these gentleman to step out?"

Naomi smiled weakly. "No, they're okay." In fact she felt rather comforted by the two old men making sure she was being cared for. It was odd, but sweet.

An hour later, after x-rays confirmed the break, and a bright neon-pink cast put on her wrist and part way up her forearm, Naomi, Sebastian, and Rooster left the hospital.

Ida Minsky

The bakery looked quite festive. She had sent Henry up to the QuikStop gas station for whatever decorations he could find and he'd come back with a Happy Birthday sign, blue and green crepe paper streamers and a packaged set of eight party hats, eight horns, and eight balloons. She had put Henry to work doing the decorations as she put the finishing touches on the birthday cake.

A smattering of friends came in, helped themselves to coffee, and began to mingle. Naomi Blue didn't have a huge group of friends, but with everyone bringing someone, the gathering became more of a community event.

Naomi Blue didn't show up.

"Henry," Ida said, pulling the boy aside. "Where is Naomi?"

"I'm not sure, Mrs. Minsky. You called her, right?"

"Yes, yes. Let's give her a little bit longer. Rooster isn't back from picking up Sebastian Skinner anyway, so let us just show some patience."

Their patience was tested for another forty minutes until Ida noticed Roger's car pull up in front of the bakery. Roger opened the door for Sebastian who got out and opened the back door—and Naomi Blue got out. Ida was surprised to find them altogether.

Naomi Blue had a cast on her arm, and the two men were both jockeying around her trying to help her out of the car, in the door, and take off her coat. Naomi looked addled, like she wasn't used to two men trying to help her so much. Amid yells of "Happy Birthday" she stood in the entrance of the bakery stunned, wearing a pair of teal colored boots.

"I'm not being fired?" Naomi asked.

NAOMI BLUE

SHE LOOKED AROUND THE BAKERY. Everyone she knew in Copper Prairie was there plus some people she'd only seen over at the Ringworm or perhaps while modeling. There were balloons tied to the ceiling and people were laughing, talking and enjoying themselves. Henry stood by the window in front of a gorgeous huge cake with way too many candles. He was smiling and clearly waiting for her to see him.

"Was this your great idea?"

"Mine and Ida's. We planned this together."

"There's no personnel matter to talk about, I bet."

"Nope. There's not."

"Wow."

Henry seemed to suddenly notice the cast. He touched her shoulder carefully.

"What happened? Where'd you get that cast?"

Naomi Blue pointed to her boots.

"Wrong boots for winter."

Henry laughed and gingerly pulled her close for a kiss. When he kissed her, there was nothing casual about it. She felt it in her toes even. She pulled back a bit and looked at him.

"What?" Henry asked. "What's wrong?"

"Thanks."

"For the party?"

"For the kiss."

"Am I interrupting anything?" Sebastian Skinner came up to Henry and Naomi, putting one arm around each of them. He smelled funny, Naomi thought. Stale.

"No, of course not. Hello, Mr. Skinner," Henry said. Naomi felt cautious—Sebastian had proven to be a bit erratic today.

"Mr. Skinner," Naomi began. "Can I ask you a few things? About this morning?"

"Tell you what, my dear. Come by the Carriage General tomorrow, and we can talk. Today is not the day. It's too noisy in here for any decent conversation and besides, I would like some cake."

Ida Minsky came over with matches and fumbled to light them. Rooster took the matches from her and quickly lit all forty candles. Naomi wondered why they had bothered with so many candles. That simply wasn't necessary, was it? The room erupted into a chorus of song after which Naomi embarrassed herself by blowing out only two-thirds of the candles. Sebastian and Rooster surprised her by leaning forward to get the rest, banging their heads over her cake. Naomi figured it was only fitting that it should be so comical. It had been a strange birthday.

Henry Alexander

Henry walked Naomi home after the party had died down. She slipped a bit as they walked—those crazy dumb boots—and he held her carefully to help her keep her balance.

This was one of those times, those rare times, when he could actually feel the shift in the relationship. He could feel it when their hands brushed. A closeness and yet still electric. They were okay. He knew it. He didn't think he'd need to tell Naomi that she wasn't too old for him. He felt sure they had moved past that. He glanced at her quickly as they walked.

"What?" she asked. "What are you looking at?"

"Nothing, just looking."

"Hmph."

Naomi unlocked the front door and walked straight to the rocking chair in the living room. Henry kneeled in front of her and silently began to pull off the teal boots. He held her feet in his hands and watched as she leaned back in the chair, closing her eyes. He was torn between wanting to carry her up the stairs and slowly undress her and love her, and thinking what she needed most was a cup of tea. They both seemed like good ideas to Henry and he hesitated, rubbing the soles of her feet.

"How about some tea, Naomi?"

"Hah. I thought you were going to suggest going upstairs."

"I was thinking it, but thought you probably needed tea more. Or would you . . ."

"Let's have tea."

Henry laughed as they went into the kitchen. He told her to sit, to let him take care of it. She didn't argue. She seemed utterly relaxed and happy to let him take care of her.

"I almost forgot," Henry said, digging in his pocket for his birthday gift for Naomi. "This is for you. Happy Birthday."

Naomi took the stone, turning it over in her hand, feeling the indent that her thumb slid into so nicely. She looked at him inquisitively. "It's beautiful, Henry."

"It's blue quartz. It's a palm stone. Some people call them worry stones. You hold it in your hand or even place it under your pillow. It's supposed to be healing. And it will reduce your anxiety."

"You think I worry too much?" Naomi laughed.

"Well, I don't want you worrying about us anymore," Henry said.

Naomi smiled and closed her eyes.

Later, Henry did try to carry her up the staircase. But it was such a narrow flight of stairs, after tottering on the fifth step, he put her down and they scrambled up the rest of the way separately. And then he carried out his earlier idea. Naomi was delightfully cooperative.

Chapter Twenty-Three

Sebastian Skinner

It was morning and Sebastian went to the store. He unlocked the back door to the Carriage General. He left the lights out, not ready to be open. He took off his boots and coat and walked about the store in his stocking feet. He realized—and the mere fact that he realized alarmed him—that this was a moment of clarity. So many years sitting on the stool by the register. So many years of trying to keep his merchandise current but not risqué, chic but not trendy. And without Wanda's presence, it no longer seemed to matter. Naomi Blue had filled the gap so well that he had not realized it. He could see Wanda emerging from the curtained dressing room and sashaying towards the mirror, knowing full well that he was watching. She always looked so good, so round in the rear, so perfect. Naomi was no Wanda. But he had let Naomi be Wanda. God, how did that happen?

He went slowly upstairs. Today, it looked less like clutter and more like a disaster had struck. Things were everywhere. He went through the center aisle towards the back. He suddenly had no energy and sat down, right there on a small area rug that someone had unrolled to look at. He sat there and cried. These weren't the tears of sweetness, nor the tears of anger, but the desperately sad tears of heartache. She was gone. It was done. Finished.

"Mr. Skinner? Are you here?" Sebastian listened to her calls. He wasn't quite ready to answer.

"Sebastian?" He remained silent.

"Mr. Skinner, I see your boots and coat, I know you're here somewhere. Are you up here?"

She sure was dammed persistent, that girl. He supposed he would answer.

"Yes, I'm up here. Just taking inventory."

"Inventory?" Naomi asked, coming upstairs. "It's awfully dark up here. Can I turn on a light?"

"No."

"No? Okay. Where are you?"

"Right here."

"Where?"

"On the floor. I'm sitting on the floor, back here."

"Oh." Naomi Blue slowly made her way through the piles of merchandise that overflowed into the center aisle.

"Join me. Sit down a spell."

"Ah, okay. Sure."

Naomi Blue sat down a few feet away from Sebastian. He felt her caution.

"Don't worry, Naomi. I'm fine."

"I'm not worried, I just don't know why we have to sit up here in the dark, that's all."

"We don't, but we will."

"Okay."

The two of them sat for a while longer in silence. Sebastian wanted to be sure his mind was together, that he wasn't going to cry in front of the girl. He was impressed that the girl knew how to sit quietly. So few young people seem to be able to tolerate a little silence.

"Naomi, I have loved having you model here at the store. You did an admirable job."

"Am I being fired?"

"No, well, yes. Well, I'm not firing you, but I think it's time to stop window modeling. I don't know that it's brought in any business."

"That's fine, Mr. Skinner. I'm fine with that. It was much harder than I'd realized it would be. Standing still is incredibly taxing, particularly when there are people watching. So don't worry about me, I'll be fine."

"Maybe you can help me out with the store, though. I think it's getting to be too much for an old man like me."

"Well, I'd have to work it out with Mrs. Minsky."

"She'll share you. I know she will. That Ida."

They sat quietly for a bit.

"But I wanted to explain something. This is odd. Awkward to explain. Quite awkward. But there were times I could have sworn you were someone else. A woman I loved. A woman I love. Only you're not. I know that. But there were times it was jumbled in my mind. Do you understand?"

"Sort of, yes."

"I have loved her for as long as I can remember. In fact, I don't remember ever not loving her. And you remind me of her, I suppose. Not really, but there are times." His voice dropped off. They sat quietly. He wasn't sure what else to say, or if he could manage to say anything more about Wanda. He had said enough.

"Tell me about the birdhouses," Naomi said softly.

"The birdhouses?"

"Yes, all those birdhouses in the shed?"

Sebastian hesitated. It was a violation of Wanda. Wanda. Her birdhouses. Lyle's birdhouses. And as quickly as that, the shutters in his mind began to close. Why was she asking about her birdhouses? She knew perfectly well about the birdhouses. Was she teasing him? Taunting him? Lyle's birdhouses.

"Sebastian?"

She was teasing him, as usual. Poking fun at him. Pretending. She knew damn well what those birdhouses were. They were Lyle's creations, Lyle's designs. But she kept them, kept them in the shed. With his poems, his notes. All those years of his words. Stuck within the chimneys, the doors, behind the perches, along the eaves, his poems were everywhere in those houses. Almost not a house without a note from him. It had gotten so difficult to slip her the notes without Lyle noticing, that eagle-eyed bastard. He took her for granted. It made him crazy. Lyle had her all the time and he himself had only the notes.

"Sebastian?"

"I'm done talking. Go now."

He sat in the dark as she went down the stairs.

Naomi Blue

Naomi opened the door to Ida's Bakery, keenly alert to the sound of the bell above the door. It was quiet within, but the smell of baking cinnamon rolls meant all was well here. Naomi walked around to the back.

"Ida?" Naomi didn't see Ida but a timer was set on the counter. Fourteen minutes remained. Naomi washed her hands and wrapped an apron on. She poured a cup of coffee, added way too much cream and sat down. She could hear the timer ticking in the silence of the bakery. Footsteps.

Ida Minsky and Rooster Robinson came down the steps into the back of the bakery with matching startled expressions when they saw Naomi sitting in front of the window. Ida fussed with her hair. Rooster adjusted his large belt buckle. Naomi felt awkward and looked back out the window.

Rooster joined Naomi with a cup of coffee while Ida checked on the ovens.

"Good morning, Naomi. How is that arm of yours?"

"It's okay, thanks. It's limiting to have a cast but it's not too painful. Just clumsy."

They sat and sipped their coffee, both angled towards the window as if they weren't really together, weren't really having a conversation.

"Can I ask you something?" Naomi ventured. Rooster glanced at Naomi and nodded.

"What's his story?"

"Whose story?"

"Sebastian Skinner. What's his story?"

"Well, there are many stories. Hard to know where to start. One story? Hah. He has many stories. Which one do you want to know?"

"I, um, I'm not sure. I guess I want to know the Wanda Cooper story."

Rooster laughed suddenly causing a bit of coffee to leak from the corner of his mouth. He quickly wiped it with the back of his sleeve.

"That's an old story. You're probably one of the few people in this town who doesn't know it. Ah, Sebastian and Wanda. Really, the story is about Sebastian and Lyle. There were rarely two better friends than those two. Too bad for Sebastian that Lyle was the one who got Wanda. Really, when they were together, the three of them, you couldn't tell which two were the couple. If you watched Sebastian's eyes, you knew he loved the girl. Lyle had a hard shell, he was one tough guy. Couldn't tell a thing from his eyes. But Sebastian wore his emotions on his sleeve like a schoolboy. He loved her. You just had to see his face to know it. The way he looked at her. Poor Sebastian. All those years. And then when Lyle passed away, she just up and moved. Down south where she didn't have to deal with these Minnesota winters we love so well."

"What about the birdhouses?"

"Birdhouses? What birdhouses? Lyle's? He had a shop in the garage where he built them. He had quite the talent for them. I used to sell them in the back of my store near the birdseed. They sold well too. Sold them to tourists in the summer. But everyone seemed to like them. Though Lyle didn't care much about them once he put in the last bit of hardware."

"So Lyle built the birdhouses."

"Yes, and then Wanda would sell them at craft fairs mostly. Nearly everyone in town probably had one at one time or another in their backyards. The Copper Prairie birds have beautiful houses, even more beautiful than the ones its residents live in." Rooster started to laugh, that laugh he had from his nose. Once it started, he didn't seem able to control it. Naomi didn't see the humor, but the fact that the very man who had the grouchiest reputation in town could so easily lose control made her start to laugh too. Ida came out from the back of the bakery curious.

"What's so funny?" she asked.

But it was too late for Rooster to answer, so immersed in his own joke. Naomi shook her head, knowing that she didn't really have an answer to that question. It just was funny.

"I'm sorry, I'm sorry," Rooster sputtered. "I don't know why that seemed so funny to me. I was just thinking about those little sparrows and chickadees enjoying Lyle's houses with the fancy shingles and spacious rooms. Such plush accommodations for such little birds. I'm sorry. It's just ridiculous." He pulled a gray bandana from his pocket and wiped his eyes.

Naomi just shook her head, smiling. It was really so simple after all. When she stopped looking so hard at the details, the big picture began quite clear. It wasn't about the birdhouses or the key. It was just about the heart.

"Hey, Mr. Robinson, do you want to split a cinnamon roll with me?" Naomi asked.

"Not a chance. I'm having my own."

Without a word, Ida went back to the counter and put three cinnamon rolls on three plates. Carefully balancing them on a round tray along with more coffee, she carried it over to the table. Rooster jumped up and got Ida a chair. She smiled at him, sitting down.

Later in the day, Naomi set out for home. She watched her step as she walked past the Ringworm, glancing in the window to see if anyone was there this early in the day. She suspected Millie Bing would be there soon, if she wasn't already there. She held her cast close to her body in a self-protection sort of way. She watched her feet on the sidewalk.

She went down Carriage Street, glancing at the Carriage General. Her window seemed empty. A single manikin posed in the corner with an empty stool in the center.

She would go back later in the week and help Sebastian Skinner set up the window with a second manikin. And she understood she would be Naomi or Wanda, depending on the day or the moment. And things like that didn't really matter anyway.

NORMANDALE COMMUNITY COLLEGE
LIBRARY
9700 FRANCE AVENUE SOUTH
BLOOMINGTON, MN 55431-4399